This all started when I watched *The Secret*! Little did I know I would sell my house, buy a boat, start a new business – 'Blue Diamond Elevation', write this book, start a YouTube channel and paint my dreams.

Co-creating with spirit is such a nurturing and uplifting experience. I love making the mundane magical, bringing a little sparkle into people's lives.

This book is dedicated to my friend John Bigglestone. Lost but not forgotten.

Claire Middleton

PIANO FINGERS

AUSTIN MACAULEY PUBLISHERS™
LONDON • CAMBRIDGE • NEW YORK • SHARJAH

Copyright © Claire Middleton 2023

The right of Claire Middleton to be identified as author of this work has been asserted by the author in accordance with sections 77 and 78 of the Copyright, Designs and Patents Act 1988.

All rights reserved. No part of this publication may be reproduced, stored in a retrieval system, or transmitted in any form or by any means, electronic, mechanical, photocopying, recording, or otherwise, without the prior permission of the publishers.

Any person who commits any unauthorised act in relation to this publication may be liable to criminal prosecution and civil claims for damages.

This is a work of fiction. Names, characters, businesses, places, events, locales, and incidents are either the products of the author's imagination or used in a fictitious manner. Any resemblance to actual persons, living or dead, or actual events is purely coincidental.

A CIP catalogue record for this title is available from the British Library.

ISBN 9781398455184 (Paperback)
ISBN 9781398455191 (ePub e-book)

www.austinmacauley.com

First Published 2023
Austin Macauley Publishers Ltd®
1 Canada Square
Canary Wharf
London
E14 5AA

I would like to thank my courageous son, Josh, for helping me find my faith and inspiring me to write.

Also, thank you Mum for listening, Dad for making me laugh in the tough times, Dan and Ross for protecting me, and Susie and Nicole for the good old days!

Finally, I'd like to thank my husband, Adam, for finding me and making my dreams come true.

Chapter 1
Heartbroken

Damien stood at the top of the spiral staircase, staring down at the grand piano that sat proudly in the living room. It had been there ever since he was a young boy but never before did he have a burning desire to play. The piano, fairly old and brown, was in very good condition for its age, giving off that cosy musty wooden smell when you first lift the cover. Around its body were beautifully etched caveman drawings which, to Damien, had always depicted a sense of freedom. Amongst the etchings were golden metal plates with inspiring words engraved, added by his mum, Clara.

The piano seemed to glow as if inviting him to its soft, comfortable stool, tempting him to place his fingers on the keys, just to see what would happen. The gold plates caught the natural light perfectly. They sparkled like diamonds in a jewellery shop window, oozing significance and luring Damien closer.

Damien stood mesmerised for a moment before the clunky sound of the front door opening brought him back to reality.

"You all right, Love? You look like you've seen a ghost."

His mum's voice seemed to echo through the hall and up

the stairs to where Damien stood, perfectly still. It was as if someone had pressed the pause button and he couldn't move. He shook his head and blinked a couple of times.

"Hi, Mum, I was just, erm... coming upstairs for something," he replied, with a somewhat bewildered expression.

Damien was a tall, stocky lad with an adorable innocence and a friendly smile. He'd just turned 22 and recently moved back in with his mum. His girlfriend, Lisa, left him two weeks ago, just after his birthday.

Clara was dashing around as usual. She was an energetic woman, always full of beans. She loved darting around here, there and everywhere. Her many different roles seemed to work alongside each other like clockwork. She had a successful photography business, mostly photographing weddings and families. She taught photography at college and did some occasional modelling, although she found it a real challenge to sit still that long and preferred being on the other side of the camera. In her twenties, she had enjoyed the fast pace and danger of her role as a retained fire fighter and more recently, had begun a new venture of painting acrylic murals on people's walls. She discovered her hidden talent with a paintbrush after an injury from a car accident left her unable to lift her camera for some time. "Variety is the spice of life," she often said and certainly lived by that.

Clara and Damien had a unique closeness. They were loving and caring towards each other and yet had a comfortable, casual demeanour like they were friends 'hanging out'. Clara often called Damien 'mate' and had done so since he was young. They lived together more like housemates than mother and son. Clara liked it this way, it felt like less pressure and growing up, Damien felt independent, which helped his confidence develop.

They'd always lived in Devizes; a cosy market town with good energy. Clara always felt safe there and never got bored of admiring the ancient buildings and churches. It was easy to imagine history in the town because the old style and worn character still shone through. Clara could see Devizes Castle from the route she walked into town. She would often stop on the bridge in the graveyard and admire the Castle's proud sense of medieval valiance. She could sometimes smell the hoppy ale drifting through the old town from Wadworths, the Brewery, and if she was really lucky, occasionally caught glimpse of the shire horses delivering barrels to the pubs. She felt privileged watching them on their rounds and enjoyed the timeless feel they brought to the quirky, classy little town.

"Well, don't forget I've got choir tonight. I might be late. I'm giving Sandy a lift home. You'll be OK, won't you? Oh look, it's six o'clock already, have you eaten?"

Choir was in Clara's favourite church by the large duck-pond they called The Crammar. She used to take Damien there when he was little and tell him the famous story about the 'Moonraker Smugglers' pretending they were raking for cheese in the water.

Damien stared blankly at her, his piercing blue eyes penetrating the silence.

"Damien? Hello? Time is getting on. Shall I chuck a pizza in?"

"Sorry…Mum. Yeah. Pizza sounds good," Damien stuttered quietly.

Clara scurried off into the kitchen, leaving Damien at the top of the stairs. A moment later, Damien resigned to his bedroom to put on an episode of 'Only Fools and Horses'. He closed his bedroom door, put on the old lamp in the corner and closed the curtains. He enjoyed the cosy feeling when it was dark. He put on his slippers and slumped into his great granddad's old brown chair in the corner of the room and reached for the TV controller.

Lisa had always said he was old before his time but Damien preferred the term 'rustically old fashioned'.

Episode five was halfway through now. Damien sat staring at the screen, expressionless. The show they used to find hilarious didn't seem funny at all. He couldn't get Lisa out of his head. The empty feeling in the pit of his stomach was like nothing he'd ever felt before.

"Damien…Pizza!!"

Just as Damien was about to go downstairs, he noticed something on the floor underneath the window. As he got closer, he could see what it was, and he felt a cold shiver run down his spine. It was a small metal keyring in the shape of a piano! Damien had no idea whose it was or how it got there but he had that strange feeling again which made him stop in his tracks.

"Damien, did you hear me? I have to go. Your pizza is down here."

Damien blinked himself back into the room again, picked up the keyring, shoved it in his jeans pocket and hurried downstairs.

"Yes, Mum, I'm coming."

Clara looked lovely in her pink dress and high heels. She'd swept her long blonde hair into some grips, revealing her elegant tanned shoulders. She always seemed to look effortlessly stylish.

"You look lovely, Mum. I hope you have a great time."

"Ah, Damien. Thank you!" Clara beamed, grateful for the compliment.

"Don't know why that idiot Lisa ever let you go. You're such a sweetheart, Damien. Now, are you going to be OK? Why don't you ask Jason around for a movie or go out for a pint? It would do you good to see your friends."

"Mum, don't worry about me. I'll be fine! Just have a good night. Say Hi to Sandy for me!"

Clara stood on tiptoes to reach Damien's cheek and gave him a peck, silently wondering where all the years had gone.

"OK. See ya!" She replied cheerfully, yet still holding a concerned look on her face.

Clara came from a close-knit family. Her mum and dad did an amazing job of instilling strong family loyalty and they all looked out for each other. Clara had an elder brother, Daniel, and a younger brother, Ross. Perhaps having two brothers was the reason for her tomboy side. She always enjoyed getting out in the woods and making dens and she loved going on crazy last-minute adventures.

Shortly after Damien was born, Clara went through some difficult times. As a single parent, Clara took on the role of both mum and dad, determined that Damien wouldn't miss out on all the stuff dads do with their sons. She used to take him for kickabouts, and they would run around tackling each other to the ground. Their favourite thing to do was to go straight to the pub from school pickup on a Friday and have a game of pool.

Facing life together helped them form a special bond and they developed a spiritual connection too. Particularly when times were hard, Clara turned to her spirituality for comfort and guidance. Damien soon picked up on this as a child and began to do the same whenever he became sad or frightened. They enjoyed chatting together about strange, spooky coincidences and Clara often called Damien her "little messenger". They used to play psychic games and always ended up laughing.

Now that Damien was an adult, their relationship couldn't be better. They supported each other and often went away on trips. Clara had an off-road motorbike and bought Damien a quad bike so that they could disappear in the country for hours.

Damien went to the fridge and found a cold beer to go with his pizza. He took them both to the cosy but spacious living room and slumped into the sofa.

"Alexa, play Fleetwood Mac."

His mum had great taste in music and over the years, Damien had developed a passion for a broad range of genres. He found comfort in lyrics, enjoyed the energy of music and seemed to connect to almost every instrument. Sometimes, it was as if the music was speaking to him.

Halfway through his favourite track *The Chain*, Damien nodded off and had the strangest dream…

Chapter 2
Signs

Clara couldn't believe it was nearly midnight. She opened the old heavy wooden door as quietly as possible and crept through the hall. Damien was asleep on the sofa. She stopped and watched him a moment, feeling proud of the man he'd become. He was a gentle lad with a quiet inner strength. She carefully tucked a blanket under his legs and pulled it up to reach his broad shoulders before heading upstairs.

The following morning when she went downstairs, he wasn't on the sofa. He was sitting at the piano, holding something in his hands.

"You all right? Were you warm enough down here?"

"Mum, I had the strangest dream. It was John. He was there. It was as if he was with me, for real, I mean. It was so vivid." Damien spoke quickly as if he was hurrying to make sense of the dream.

"John? You saw John in your dreams? Wow! I told you, he's still with you."

"He was trying to tell me something, Mum, give me a message but the post came through the door and woke me up, and I missed what he was trying to tell me."

Clara walked over and put a hand on Damien's shoulder.

"I'm sorry, sweetheart. He will find a way to get his message to you. Don't worry. What's that you're holding?"

"It's a keyring. It was on my floor by the window yesterday. Have you seen it before?"

"Never. Why, is it not yours?"

"No, I don't know where it came from and yesterday, I had a weird feeling when I was looking at this old piano."

"Oooooo…maybe it's a sign!"

For as long as Damien could remember, Clara had a mystical approach to life and always openly spoke of signs and guidance she thought were being sent for her. Once, when she was with Damien's dad, she had a premonition and jumped up as they were falling asleep one night, telling him he must drive extra carefully to work the next day. Sure enough, he rang her from work the following day, telling her of a deer that jumped out in front of his car, forcing him off the road!

"Mum! You and your signs!"

"Well, why did you mention it if you don't think it's a sign?"

"I don't know! It's probably nothing. My head's all over the place. I better go. I'm meeting Jason for a catch-up."

"Oh good, I'm so glad. Have a good one. I'll see you tonight. I'll cook a curry, yeh?" Damien and Clara loved a curry. Clara could still remember when Damien was a toddler and had just started talking; he used to sit in the trolley in the supermarket pointing at the poppadoms, saying "cuyyeee niiight".

"Yeah, sure. Thanks, Mum."

As Damien left the house and made his way down the street, he noticed that the air felt crisp and fresh. The sky was bright and there was that lovely autumnal smell. He loved the smell of a turning season. Autumn was his favourite time of the year. He was particularly fond of September, when the leaves were just beginning to turn. One of his favourite things about autumn was putting on his old walking boots and taking long walks, kicking the leaves and smelling the fresh air, enjoying the occasional whiff of a distant bonfire. The smell of smoke always reminded him of long days in the garden with his mum. They'd stay out sitting by the fire all evening sometimes, just chatting. Occasionally, Mum would make them vegetable soup on the hob when they got indoors. The perfect end to a day outside all huddled up, the soup bowl warming his cold fingers.

Damien crossed the road and took a left onto Topslow Avenue, where his friend Jason lived. He could see Jason perched on the wall outside his house, looking down at his iPod. Jason shared Damien's love of old music and it seemed to be an escape for him too. Damien knew when everything had become a bit too much for Jason because he'd be listening to Pink Floyd. 'Delicate Sound of Thunder' was his go-to album when he wanted to make sense of life.

Jason always seemed to make sure he was out front when Damien arrived. Damien sometimes wondered what he was hiding. They'd been friends for years now, yet he had only met Jason's family once. Jason never spoke about them and seemed to go out of his way to avoid encounters.

"All right, mate."

"Hey, what's up?"

"Long time no see."

"Yeah, sorry, man. My head's all over the shop; you know how it is," Damien replied, determined to avoid delving into too much detail.

"I know, buddy. It's tough. Hang on in there, mate. Time's a healer and all that. Where are we going anyway, Christie's?"

Christie's was their place to hang out. It was a bar-come-coffee shop, really quirky with a friendly atmosphere. They always felt welcome there. The pair might look like a couple of strong blokes who could put up a fight but they were both quite sensitive, vulnerable lads, never after any trouble and liked to keep to themselves. Christie's was perfect. It had a lot of little cubby holes with comfy sofas and low lighting, great if you're not in the mood for the general public. Then there was the bar with those tall wooden stools for when you're feeling a little bolder. Sometimes, they sat there with a pint and chatted to Cindy, the short red-headed lady with a squawky voice. Today was definitely a 'cubby hole comfy sofa' day.

"What ya havin, mate? It's on me today," Jason said warmly.

"Ah, cheers, Jase. I'll have a pint of 6X."

"A pint of 6X and a Kronenbourg, please," Jason ordered, and then laughing, turned to Damien. "I don't know how you can drink that stuff."

"I've got grandad to thank for that. He used to let me have a sneaky mouthful when Mum wasn't looking. I must have got a taste for it."

The pair found a corner and started chatting about music. Jason was a keen guitarist and was trying to convince Damien to learn bass so they could jam together. Damien's response was always the same, "Not a musical bone in my body. Just doesn't come naturally to me".

The truth was Damien had never actually tried to play anything. He didn't realise that the years he'd spent developing his musical passion, by listening to and feeling the music, was the groundwork for creating his own.

He'd not yet taken a sip of his pint when Damien noticed something moving in the shadows under the table opposite theirs. He stared, trying to see more than his eyes would allow, until finally as if lured out by Damien's stare, a black cat wandered out of the darkness towards him. It had a strange look about it. It looked scared yet menacing, coy yet aggressive. It had jet black eyes that almost disappeared into its black fur.

Damien continued to stare at the cat, which sat by his feet and stared right back at him as if daring him to look away first.

"Looks like you've got a friend there," Jason piped up out of nowhere.

Damien jerked his gaze away from the cat, feeling inhibited.

"Oh, guess what?" Jason continued. "Mum's only gone and got us a dog! It's a cocker-something, looks a bit like 'lady' off that film, Lady and the Tramp. She's called it Love! Love of all things! She reckons it's going to bring Love to the family! She's gone mad, mate!"

"Wow." Damien blurted, more amazed that Jason had mentioned his mum than the fact that they had got a dog!

As the lads chatted away, the empty-pit feeling in Damien's stomach lifted slightly, giving him a little breathing space from his broken heart. They finished their drinks and were heading home when Jason suddenly remembered.

"Ahh, I need a guitar string. Can we just go to Jerry's on the way back?"

Jerry's was a music shop on the corner, only two streets away from where Jason lived.

"Yeah, course we can." Damien liked looking around Jerry's too.

As the pair walked in, the old-fashioned bell above the door seemed to bring Damien into the moment purposely. He closed the door behind him and couldn't help but notice how bright it was in the shop. Much brighter than outside which was slightly overcast now.

The light in the shop appeared to be coming from a room towards the back of the building. Damien started to make a beeline for the room as if his legs were in charge.

When he got to the doorway, he froze. He stood rooted to the floor, paralysed. The only thing that moved was his jaw as it dropped open.

Chapter 3
An Introduction to Faith

Melanie was a sweet girl of 16. With short pink hair and a quirky style, she dressed confidently. Sometimes she experimented with tie-dying her clothes and tearing bits off here and there to spruce up an outfit. Working at the local animal adoption centre suited Melanie down to the ground. She loved taking care of all the animals and often wanted to take them home. Today was no exception! A white rabbit named 'Faith' had been brought in by the gentleman down the road, who found the bunny sitting on the pavement. Apparently, he was able to pick him up without much of a struggle from the rabbit, which was most unusual. Melanie couldn't take her eyes off the rabbit's beautiful golden eyes. She'd never seen a colour like this on an animal or any being for that matter, yet it looked perfectly natural.

Brenda, the owner of the rescue centre was a popular member of the local community, with such a gentle, caring nature. Melanie's mum was so glad when Brenda had asked her daughter to work part-time at the centre because Melanie found great comfort in animals and seemed to communicate with them on a different level than most people. Her mum always knew she was gifted and that in the right place, surrounded by the right people, Melanie could accomplish extraordinary things. She hadn't gone to a mainstream school because she had dyslexia, which made it difficult for her to get the most out of lessons. Her mum took the brave decision to homeschool her, and she began to flourish. They found private tutors for the subjects Melanie wanted to study. One of her favourite topics was photography. She seemed to have a talent for it and looked forward to capturing nature at every opportunity.

It was Christmas time when Melanie and her mum met Clara. They both enrolled in Clara's photography course at the local college. Melanie still remembered sitting in the classroom on the first day, watching Clara dash around the room with a kind of nervous but upbeat energy. Clara was very professional and switched on, yet she also had a slightly scatty nature. That's what Melanie liked about her.

After the course, Clara started tutoring Melanie at her home, and the pair went on a couple of trips together, taking photos in the city. They soon became close. Clara enjoyed their time together. Melanie reminded her of the young photographer she once was, so inspired and curious about every aspect of photography. They even set up a darkroom at Melanie's home with the enlarger that Clara had in her loft.

When Melanie told Clara that she had achieved the top grade at GCSE Photography and that she was going to college, Clara couldn't have been prouder. She hoped that one day they would work together.

"You love the new addition, don't you, dear?" Brenda called from out the back, where they kept all the animal food. Brenda was a short plump lady in her sixties. She had lovely olive skin, blonde hair and a kind smile.

"He's gorgeous!" Melanie screeched, secretly wondering how she could get her mum to fall in love with the rabbit too!

Melanie had a shy, gentle nature. She was quite timid around most people but not with Brenda. They'd known each other for years. Melanie's mum used to stop and chat with Brenda while she was walking her to school. Brenda always managed to find a couple of coins in her handbag to give to Melanie for her moneybox.

"I don't think your mum is going to want any more pets, love!" Brenda called back as if reading Melanie's mind.

Melanie took the bunny under her arm and hugged him tightly. She found some grass and dandelion leaves and put her in a run with the other rabbits and guinea pigs. The guinea pigs always started squeaking whenever Melanie went near them as if they were chatting away with her.

Just as she was about to find them some fresh hay, Melanie heard Brenda calling her name. She sounded somewhat frantic. Melanie dashed inside.

"What the…" Melanie gasped.

Brenda was sitting on the floor, holding a box she'd found on the doorstep. Inside the box was a baby lion! A real-life baby lion, as if it had just stepped out of the circus!

"You're not keeping this one!" Brenda laughed.

Melanie giggled, staring at the lion in disbelief. "Look, there's a name tag!" She gently moved close to take a look.

Melanie turned over the gold nametag and read aloud "Pride".

"A lion called Pride! Wow!"

Brenda was about to pick up the unusually calm and harmless-looking cat when she stopped and just watched. It was most peculiar; the cat didn't seem fazed at all. It seemed as if it was exactly where it needed to be. Brenda heard a knock on the back door. She pulled open the door and the local policeman, Steve, was standing in the courtyard, holding the most beautiful white barn owl Brenda had ever seen.

Steve looked almost as shocked as Brenda. "Got room for one more?" He said, trying to sound playfully dismissive. He seemed taller than usual today. At six feet two, Steve towered over Brenda. He was a slim chap, really friendly and fancied himself as a bit of a ladies' man. Sometimes, Brenda wondered if he overdid the charm to cover his clumsy side.

"Steve, what's going on?"

"I can't say too much. You know how it is."

"Oh, please! Steve, you've known me for years, come on! I've just found a lion cub on the doorstep and now you turn up with an owl!"

"OK, but keep it to yourself. There are a lot of frightened people…"

"Frightened?" Brenda cut in.

"Yes, there have been a few sightings of strange things. And this owl, well, it's a bit odd too. An elderly man approached a lad down the street. He's been described as having a long white beard and a shaky jaw. If you see him, please call us. He handed this owl to the lad and was muttering 'Purity Purity' over and over. Then he vanished. I saw the lad myself. He was quite shaken."

Brenda put a hand up to stroke the owl's wing. She didn't know what to say. The owl seemed so calm and tame. It was almost as if the owl had come home, it seemed perfectly at ease.

"Can you manage this?" Steve asked, looking hopeful.

"Of course, yes!"

Steve handed over the owl and said goodbye.

Brenda stood a while, holding the owl and looking deep into its beautiful golden eyes. It seemed like the world stopped for a moment. As she held her gaze, the owl didn't move or look away as if silently trying to tell her something. It was mesmerising.

Brenda suddenly felt unusually aware of her surroundings. The air was musty yet fresh, the sky seemed almost orange and she could hear children playing in the distance; she heard Melanie chatting with the lion and the gentle hum of the air-con unit. Brenda felt rooted to the ground and wanted to just 'be' for a moment to take it all in.

Melanie called out, breaking the stillness. "Brenda, are you OK? What are you doing out there?"

Brenda came back to earth. "I'm coming, dear, wait until you see this…"

Chapter 4
The Golden Glow
of Consciousness

Damien went from being paralysed to being pulled further into the room full of golden light. His legs seemed to move before his brain told them to.

Looking thoroughly out of place, in the centre of the small tired-looking room with old wallpaper and chipped white paint, was an immaculate gold piano, glowing as if from another world. Its glow lit the whole room, piercing through the musty atmosphere with yellow beams of light.

He sat on the stool at the piano immersed in golden light. The light seemed to sparkle with magic as if there was gold glitter floating all around him. He was suddenly aware of his weight on the stool, his body temperature and he could hear every sound, from the people talking in the next room to the buzz of the lightbulb above his head. The slightly damp smell in the room was fused with sweet cinnamon. He could feel his heart beating in his chest. His feet felt as if they were rooted deeply into the earth. A new level of consciousness had risen within him.

Damien just sat, taking in this new environment for a few

minutes, connecting every sense deeply to his surroundings. It felt as if he had fresh eyes. He was 'seeing' for the first time. He was awake.

What was happening? Damien's stream of thoughts began. Had he been sleepwalking through life up until now? What had he missed out on? Was this normal? Was it going to end? Was it a gift from God? Was he being sent an insight into how life could be if he were fully conscious?

As his stream of thoughts continued, Damien noticed the golden light fading around him. The sparkle and glitter were dimming, and the piano didn't seem to glow as brightly. He was less aware of every sensation in his body too. He started to feel disappointment rising inside him. He wanted the magical golden glow to stay, he wanted to keep his new eyes but the more he feared losing it, the more the good feeling poured out of him.

Within minutes, Damien found himself sitting at a brown, worn-looking piano in a dimly lit room. It was gone. Was it magic? Whatever it was, Damien wanted it back. Everything felt safer in the golden light; life sparkled again.

Damien got up and half staggering out of the room, he stopped to look back in disbelief at the old piano. He caught up with Jason, who was paying for his guitar string.

"You all right, Damo?" Jason said, trying to figure out the unfamiliar expression on Damien's face. Before Damien got a chance to respond, they were interrupted.

"Hey! Damien!" The cheerful voice Damien knew so well came from behind him. It was Damien's uncle, Ross.

"All right, Ross! How you doing? Don't tell me you're buying another guitar?"

Ross just smiled and shrugged. At six feet five, Ross had

the height and physique of a sports model. He was tanned and toned and always looked well. Damien thought he was the coolest guy around. He was the guy even the bad lads liked. He seemed to have everyone's respect wherever he went. He had trained as a sports therapist and recently put a name to his own business 'Origins Sports Therapy'.

"I am so jealous, man!" Jason piped up from behind Damien.

"Jason, my man! How's it going? You nailed that riff yet?" Ross loved chatting music with Jason and enjoyed giving him tips.

"Getting there slowly! Every time I go on 'Beeywoy', I wanna give up! Your videos are addictive, though!" Beeywoy was Ross' YouTube channel. Jason's favourite videos were of Ross playing parts of 'Stairway to Heaven', 'Bohemian Rhapsody' and 'Wish You Were Here'.

"No way! Never give up! You're awesome! Come around some time for a jam!"

"Ah yeah, I'd love to! Cheers!"

"And I'll see you soon, Damien. Tell your mum I'll pop around soon for a catch-up."

"Yeah, sure. She'll like that."

Damien high-fived his uncle and followed Jason out of the shop, barely noticing the ring of the bell as they left. The air seemed cooler now, and the sky was an eerie grey with an orange tint. They walked in silence for a few minutes. Jason was pondering over the conversation with Ross. When he looked up at Damien, he noticed he still had a slightly troubled expression on his face. Jason nervously asked, "So, have you seen Lisa since, you know?"

The sound of her name sent pain through Damien's chest,

and the empty feeling in his stomach returned in an instant.

"No, mate. It's like I never existed. What am I going to do now? My whole future had her in it."

"Ah, sorry, man. I don't know what to say. What about work? Can you throw yourself into it? It would be a good distraction."

"Maybe, when I get my head straight. There just seems no point to anything without her."

Damien had trained as a plumber after he left school and had recently started taking on his own clients. He loved working for himself and was excited about the future. He wanted to secretly put some money aside to surprise Lisa and suggest buying a house together. She worked as a freelance hairdresser and always wanted a cottage in the country with a big garden and ducks.

Jason didn't know how to console Damien and kept thinking he was saying the wrong thing, making his friend feel worse. But Damien just appreciated seeing a friendly face and having a reason to get out of the house.

"Thanks for today, mate." Damien broke the silence.

Jason was about to respond when both lads stopped dead. They stood, staring in disbelief.

Chapter 5
A Horse Called Strength

Jeremy was a strong, stocky lad, with a huge smile stretching across his sweet round face. He was from a hardworking and wealthy family; the down-to-earth kind that weren't too caught up in their success. They lived in a beautiful house in the country and kept all sorts of animals from horses to quail.

Mrs Burgess, Jeremy's mum was a well-spoken lady. She ran a business from home making pyjamas. It was always healthily chaotic in the Burgess household, with people coming and going, building projects on the go, cake sales, and plenty of family gatherings when Jeremy's family visited from London. Mr Burgess, a lawyer, spent much of his time in his office or on the road, travelling from case to case.

Jeremy had such a good heart. He wanted to help people and was especially passionate about helping the homeless. He volunteered in a homeless shelter and worked for the police carrying out admin tasks. He loved to work, loved being around people, and had so much to give. The life and soul of the party, he was like a ray of sunshine and had a special way of making people laugh. Everyone in the area knew of Jeremy. He was often spotted dancing down the street with his headphones on, singing loudly with a huge smile on his face.

"Mum, I'm taking Strength out for a trot," Jeremy said, peeping over his glasses, hoping there were no more chores to do.

"OK, Jeremy," Mrs Burgess said in an assertive but warm tone, "see you later. I'm cooking cottage pie for your supper."

"Mum, you are spectacular, my favourite person in the world," replied Jeremy, meaning every word.

Jeremy named his new horse Strength because he always felt strong inside when he was with him. They would disappear for hours together, through the forest and over the hills. The gentle horse never expected anything of him, never judged him. They were best friends.

Jeremy was a happy lad but his Down syndrome always seemed to hold him back from living the life he dreamed of. He had so much passion for music, dance and performing arts and wished he could somehow work doing what he loved. Sometimes it made him angry. He used to say to his support worker, Janice, "I don't want Down syndrome anymore".

It broke Janice's heart when he said this. She just wanted to make everything better for him.

Jeremy frequently went from feeling gifted to feeling cursed. His wonderful zest for life and passion for people was shadowed by his frustration, his yearning for a 'normal' life and his dreams feeling out of reach.

Janice was convinced that Jeremy had a special place in this world; they only had to find it. The pair enjoyed adventures together, from visiting homeless shelters to going for long country walks.

"Good boy. I love you, Strength. You are my incredible best friend. You make me feel magical."

Jeremy and Strength headed down the lane and across the

field towards the forest. Strength seemed to know exactly where to stop so that Jeremy could admire the lake. He laid his head down on the horse's neck and hugged him with both arms and legs. They stayed there a while, just wandering around, exploring every inch of the water's edge. Time went so fast when Jeremy was out with Strength.

The sky seemed a strange orange colour and the woods by the lake felt a little different today.

"It's spooky here," Jeremy whispered in Strength's ear, feeling a little uneasy.

They began to make their way back home. From the top of the hill, Jeremy could see for miles. The orange sky seemed to loom over him. The dark grey clouds looked particularly menacing as if threatening the orange fog. Clara's older brother, Daniel, and his fiancé, Jayne, came wandering towards him and Jeremy was glad to see the familiar faces.

"Hello there, Jeremy," Daniel said in his formal manner.

"D-Dan and J-Jayne, hello!" Jeremy stuttered. "My horse, Strength is looking after me."

"Excellent! I'm glad to hear it!" Daniel and Jayne often took long walks in the country together. Jayne found that the country inspired her artistic side. She'd been working on some incredible paintings of animals she hoped to exhibit soon.

"How's business?" Jeremy asked, enjoying a 'normal' conversation with Daniel.

"Yes," Daniel replied, sounding more posh than Jeremy remembered, "I sold two guitars this week." Daniel had his own guitar building business. He loved the freedom of working from home and enjoyed the jamming sessions with Ross, putting the new guitars to test before he sold them.

"That's fantastic!" Jeremy said cheerfully, not at all intimidated by Daniel's professional tone. There was a long pause before Jeremy continued. "It is s-so good to see you both. I am going to gallop away now and eat Mum's pie for dinner."

Daniel and Jayne both smiled and said goodbye to Jeremy. "You take care," Jayne added warmly.

Jeremy gave Strength a gentle nudge and bent his head low, enjoying his speed. He was soon glad to be home. He led Strength safely to his stable, enjoying the faint smell of Mum's cooking. With a warmed appetite, he bounced eagerly towards the house. As he reached the old wooden gate, he thought he saw something on the path ahead. Deciding it must have been a trick of the light, he carried on, feeling hungry.

It was then that it happened.

Chapter 6
Fear Meets Love

Clara loved getting her hair cut, mostly because she had such a connection with her hairdresser, Bronwyn. They'd become particularly close since Clara had her long blonde locks cut right off short and donated them to the Little Princess Trust. Bronwyn knew how much Clara loved her hair; she'd been growing it for years. Bronwyn was nervously giggling with apprehension the day she cut it all off.

"What we doing this time, then?" Bronwyn asked now, always looking a little nervous.

"I need a killer haircut, mate! I'm going to be famous!"

The laughter began. Bronwyn loved it when Clara came in. She just couldn't wait to hear 'the next chapter' of Clara's life. After a quick chat, the girls decided on a sleek new style for Clara, and Bronwyn started washing her hair, eager to hear the next instalment.

"So…romance first. What's happening with Toby?"

Clara and Toby had been dating for a year now. They'd known about one another a long time, and last year, Toby got in touch and asked Clara out. Clara had told Toby she was on a 'spiritual journey' and didn't want anything romantic but a "coffee between friends wouldn't hurt". Little did she know they'd have so much to talk about! They could chat away for hours and very quickly, there was a chemistry between them. They shared a passion for music and most special of all, he made Clara laugh.

Clara began giving Bronwyn a quick update on the love life when Bronwyn seemed to detect the romance gossip just wasn't that juicy and like a hungry wolf, quickly moved onto the next subject, knowing there was only so far she could drag out this haircut.

"OK...so, so, so, the dream house? What's going on? What was it called again, May-something?" Bronwyn's eyes were wide. It had been too long since these two caught up.

"Mayfield! It's still on the market! It's waiting for me, right?" Clara exclaimed before continuing with rising excitement. "Seriously, it's mental, what's going on. I don't know where to start! I need to write it all down someday, so I don't forget!"

"Clara! Get on with it!"

"OK, sorry," Clara continued, laughing. "So, you know I sold the house and I'm renting? Well, I started seeing other places, thinking I could buy one, do it up a bit quick, then get it back on the market, so I put an offer in on a place. I didn't get it, then it came back on the market, by which time I didn't want it..." Bronwyn's eyes darted as she kept up with Clara's increasingly fast-paced and slightly jumbled story.

"Then, I got a message from, you know, up there, saying don't let go of the dream!"

'The dream' was born when Clara had been mucking around on Rightmove about a year ago after another painful breakup and saw a beautiful place she could never afford. She showed Damien the photos and joked about winning the money to buy the house. They chatted about their dream home they'd have one day, and both agreed it would have a sensory room, a log cabin in the garden, a chemical-free pool and a stained-glass window.

About a week later, Clara's mum, Helen, a gifted artist, sent Clara a painting, and she'd written the words 'Listen to your heart' on it. Helen usually painted to raise money for animal sanctuaries and wasn't particularly spiritual, so when she told Clara she "had a strong urge to send it to her", Clara knew it meant something. Clara sat and meditated, focusing on 'listening to her heart'. In an instant, she knew it was about the house she'd seen on Rightmove. She grabbed the phone, rang the estate agents, and booked a viewing. Of course, the estate agents probably thought she was wasting their time but when Clara saw the stained-glass window in the house's hallway, she let out a gasp and knew this was going to be an adventure.

Clara went home and told Damien all about the house. "We need to watch 'The Secret' again!" She told him. 'The Secret' was a DVD all about the law of attraction and how, when you ask the universe for what you want, believe it will happen, and live through gratitude every day, your dream will come to you.

Clara never thought she would sell her home she'd worked so hard on but holding onto a quote from the secret 'you don't have to see the whole staircase, just take the first step', she put her place on the market and had a buyer within a week!

Clara kept a photo of the dream house under the tree that Christmas and visualised herself there every day. She had a vision of the house being a place of healing for people who were struggling. She had recently signed up for an online course to become a strategic intervention life coach. She wanted to help people to make positive changes in their lives, find their purpose and follow their dreams.

The time was coming when she'd have to move out and nothing miraculous had happened with the dream house. But she knew it would come. She agreed on a date her buyers could move in and told Damien they'd be leaving soon.

"Where are we going to live?" Damien asked.

"Who knows, isn't it exciting?" Clara found it hard to cope with ordinary life sometimes. It was like she had to make everything extraordinary to give her courage. She got four pieces of paper and started scribbling on them.

"Oh no!" Damien said, knowing what was coming.

"Pick one! Whatever it says, we will do, wholeheartedly."

Clara had written 'buy a boat', 'buy some land and a caravan', 'rent a place' and 'travel until something comes up' on the pieces of paper. Damien was always up for an adventure and loved his mum's outlook. He closed his eyes and picked a piece of paper.

"Rent a place," he said.

Surprised yet somewhat relieved he didn't pick 'boat', Clara found a place to rent and here they are.

Bronwyn was just cutting Clara's fringe, so she knew time was running out.

Clara started speaking even faster. "So, anyway, I had this crazy inspiration to write a spiritual self-help book. A while ago, Mum told me she thought I should write a book of my poems and I wanted to but it seemed daunting. Anyway, I started it, and all this knowledge from everything I've learned to do with self-help came flooding back. My fingers couldn't keep up with my brain. Then, it gets better; I fell asleep for about ten minutes one afternoon and had this crazy dream. I woke up and instantly started writing! It was the opening of a novel! A novel! Me! Writing a novel!"

Bronwyn's face was alive with excitement and the energy in the salon was buzzing. "You've given me goosebumps, look!" She said, holding her arm to where Clara could see.

"That's not all! I went for a massage and met the characters of the book!"

"What?"

Bronwyn shook with the tingle down her spine. "This is on a whole new level. You know that, don't you?"

"I know it is crazy! But look, we've only talked about me."

"I love it, though," Bronwyn said, meaning it. "I just love it."

Bronwyn and Clara stared at each other for a few seconds, thoroughly inspired, wanting to carry on and on and chat all day.

"When shall I book in again? I'm growing it but we will need another catch-up!"

"Eight weeks?"

"Perfect! Let's book two slots so we have longer to chat!"

The girls laughed, said goodbye, and Clara headed out of the salon feeling fantastic.

She had just turned the corner into Topslow Avenue when she spotted Damien and Jason up ahead. They were running after a dog and shouting "Love". That wasn't all. A big black cat was chasing the dog and the boys were trying to stop it.

Damien spotted Clara and instantly shouted, "Mum! Help!"

Chapter 7
The Pandemic

Clara ran towards Damien and Jason. Damien looked genuinely scared.

"Mum, quick. Stop that cat."

The black cat was chasing Jason's dog, Love. The cat was hissing and scratching at his legs.

Clara ran after them and somehow managed to get between the cat and dog. The dog ran to Jason, whimpering.

"What was that all about?" Clara asked, not expecting the response she got.

"We came out of Jerry's, and they were everywhere."

"What were?"

"Black cats! The sky went a weird colour and all these cats started to appear. We got to Jason's and he was showing me his new dog when this cat came out of nowhere and started attacking the poor thing."

Clara didn't know what to make of it all but could see it had shaken Damien up.

"Is Love hurt?" she asked.

Love was sitting between Jason's legs. "He's just frightened, I think. I'm going to take him inside. I'll see you soon, Damo, yeah?"

"OK, mate, see ya."

Clara took Damien's arm and tried to think of something positive to say.

"D'you like my hair? It's ready for when I'm famous."

Damien smiled warmly but didn't say anything.

"Bronwyn recons our dream house is coming! Hold on in there, Love. It's going to be great!"

Damien had his own dreams of buying a place with Lisa and this just reminded him of his loss. He tried not to let it show.

"You better get on and finish that book then, before the dream house gets sold to someone else!"

"Yes, yes, I will! I needed a couple of days to get out and recharge, that's all. Anyway, what about that book you started writing? The one with the venom-thingies?"

"The venom vapers! Yeah, fair one. I will finish it one day."

Damien had started writing a book before Lisa broke up with him. It was about a wizard named Andy Silke, and the story was based on a war between good and evil.

But since the breakup, Damien had no inspiration to keep writing.

"Perhaps we should write together. It will give us both a kick up the bum," Clara said enthusiastically.

"Maybe when I'm feeling a bit better," Damien replied flatly.

"Maybe writing will make you feel better," Clara said sharply, not meaning to be impatient. "Sorry, I just want you to be OK."

"I will be, Mum, don't worry. Let's get a takeaway tonight, yeah?"

"I'm definitely up for that!" Clara said, glad she wouldn't have to cook.

Damien let them into the house and went upstairs for a shower.

"I'll go and get tea. What are you having? The usual?"

"Yeah, great. Thanks, Mum. My shout tonight."

"You get next week's, I've got this." Clara got changed into her comfy clothes and headed to the local Indian restaurant.

It was unusually quiet in town, and the restaurant was empty. Clara was glad. It meant she would get home to the sofa with her takeaway faster. Takeaway night was a real treat for Clara and Damien because they were careful not to make it too much of a habit. They always looked forward to it. They made it a bit of an event; sometimes they put a movie on with it or enjoyed a beer together with some music.

Clara was just pulling away and felt an urge to put the radio on. She'd just caught the end of the six o'clock news and the gist of what she was hearing didn't sound good. At first, she wasn't fully listening but she heard the word "pandemic" followed by a warning, which sounded more like an order, not to go outside.

As Clara drove through the town, she noticed the streets were empty. There wasn't a single person to be seen, not even in the pub windows which were usually alive with groups of chatting friends enjoying the start of the weekend. Clara pulled into the marketplace and stopped for a moment to take it in. The square looked beautifully untouched. The warm gentle glow of the street lights against the old-fashioned etched stone made it picture perfect. The large stone fountain flowing with glistening water sat proudly against the backdrop of a softly lit evening sky. The empty benches and piercing silence gave the pretty town that Christmas Day feeling, like the streets were finally getting a well-earned rest from trampling feet and restless rushing souls.

Was something trying to wake us up? To show us the beauty all around that we miss? Clara slowly started driving out of the marketplace towards home. She began reflecting on that nagging feeling she often got, that she had been sleepwalking through life, brainwashed by society. The sight of the empty town had come as a reminder to Clara, to wake up, to keep believing in something bigger, to follow her intuition and stay conscious.

Clara pulled into Rudlow Street and onto her driveway, feeling unsettled but without fear. When she got out of the car, she saw five black cats, sitting and watching her. They had a strange look about them. Some of them looked scared and the others looked like they were waiting to pounce and attack.

Clara scurried inside and called Damien instantly.

"You OK, Mum?" He could sense confusion in his mum's expression. "What's up?"

"I just caught the end of the news; they were warning people not to go outside. The town was empty."

"There's something strange going on, Mum, those cats. I know it sounds crazy but it just felt so weird. Do you think there's a connection?"

"I don't know," Clara replied, deliberately not mentioning the cats she saw outside their house.

Clara and Damien snuggled up on the sofa with their takeaway and a blanket. Instead of a movie, they put the radio on, hoping to catch some news.

"Hello. I'm Bessie Cartright. There appears to be a

pandemic of fear spreading throughout the country. There are reports of animals acting strangely and sightings of black cats in large numbers. These cats seem to be hostile. There have been attacks on family pets and in some cases, people. Until the government understands more, the advice is to stay inside for your safety."

Clara and Damien looked at each other in disbelief. Neither of them said a word. There wasn't much to say with such little information. They sat for the rest of the evening listening to music, both feeling uneasy. Finally, Clara broke the silence between them.

"I'm going to hit the sack. Night, mate. Love you."

"Night, Mum. Thank you for the curry. Love you too."

Damien followed shortly afterwards. He laid on his bed and fell into a restless sleep.

Chapter 8
Piano Fingers

The beautiful sound of a distant melody woke Clara.

She put on her dressing gown and groggily walked towards the spiral staircase, following the music.

When she saw where the music was coming from, she couldn't believe her eyes. It was Damien playing! He'd never played a single note on the piano before, yet there he was, sitting at the piano, playing the most serene, gentle music. The piano looked more beautiful than ever and the golden etched plate reading 'believe' appeared to glow beyond measure.

Clara sat on the bottom step and watched her son in admiration. He looked completely relaxed and hadn't noticed she was there. He came to the end of what he was playing and sat in silence. Clara noticed that the expression on his face was also one of surprise.

"Damien, that was beautiful!"

Damien jumped and turned to Clara, who was still sitting on the stairs.

"Mum. It's John. I had a dream, and he was there. It's what he was trying to tell me the other night. He got the message to me, Mum. He said, 'Piano Fingers!'"

Clara didn't look overly surprised because she was used

to receiving messages from spirit.

"Wow! You're meant to play the piano!"

"But how? How can I play like that, just out of nowhere?"

"You're in the moment. You're connected, sweetheart. When we connect to spirit and go beyond the limited confines of the mind, we discover gifts we didn't know we had."

"Oh, now I understand about you writing that book, Mum!"

"Yes, and I'm going to do some more writing today. I've realised it's not just meditating that helps creativity flow, it works the other way too. Our flowing creativity helps us in meditation. Since I've been writing that book, I've noticed I'm more conscious in everyday life."

Clara was making sense of things as she spoke.

"Maybe it's because when I'm writing, I'm not thinking about anything else. I'm completely immersed in what I'm doing. It's almost a meditation in itself. So, my mind is naturally becoming more focused. It's like I'm seeing with new eyes. What's up?" Clara asked when she saw Damien's expression suddenly change.

"You said new eyes."

"Yes. It's like seeing for the first time."

The memory of the golden piano in the music shop was back in an instant. Damien had been trying to figure out what it was about since it happened but now he understood. It was about consciousness, being awake, taking it all in. He realised it was the stream of thoughts that made the sparkly feeling disappear because they took him out of feeling the moment and back into the chaos of his busy mind. It all made sense.

"Mum, thank you so much!"

"What for?"

Damien explained what had happened at Jerry's, and Clara hugged him.

"You've been given a gift, Damien. A glimpse of how you can feel. Meditate, play the piano. Do whatever makes you happy and in the moment. You will awaken and it will heal your broken heart."

"John is helping me, Mum. He knew. He knew playing the piano would make me feel good again. It's like he knows me better now than he did when he was alive."

"That's because he's closer to you now. And he can see straight into your soul and knows what will help you connect to it."

"This stuff about connecting to your soul, I've heard you say about this before. Can you explain it again?" Damien asked with keen new interest.

Clara explained what Brahma Kumaris had taught her. That the soul's original qualities are peace, love, joy, happiness and truth. In this troubled world, we collect unwanted negativity such as fear and anxiety, anger and stress, jealousy, attachment, greed, and lust. We begin to live life through these and lose touch with our soul, our authentic self. Raja yoga meditation, focusing on the original qualities of the soul helps you drop the unwanted negative traits and free yourself from the pain they bring.

"Wow!" Damien said, hopefully. "So, we've all become kind of possessed by the negativity?"

"Exactly. And for some people, it's a lifelong habit of thinking negatively and struggling with depression. But there is a way out."

"I can see why you want to help people, Mum, you've learned so much. I think you can help a lot of people."

"I hope so. Have you heard any news this morning?"

"No. I don't listen to the news first thing in the morning since you told me to be careful what I absorb when I first wake up and the last thing before bed. Only laughter and inspirational stuff, remember?"

"Oh yes! Glad you were listening!"

The Miracle Morning book was a life-changer for Clara. She still lived by certain attitudes she developed reading that book. It explains that how you spend the first 30 minutes of your day sets the tone for the whole day! If you get up late, feeling rushed and stressed, chances are you will feel that way to some degree for most of the day. When you get up with purpose and sit in calm stillness, you are much more likely to feel a sense of calm throughout the day.

"Seeing you sitting at this piano, I reckon your day will have an inspired feel to it!"

"You bet! I'm excited! I might even get some piano books and learn properly!"

It was so good to see Damien come alive. Clara realised it was the first time in a long while that he looked motivated. She left him to it and went upstairs to her sensory room, the perfect place to work on her book.

Damien, still sitting at the piano, ordered some piano books and one on meditation. Remembering what his mum had said, he began to focus on the qualities of his soul. He remembered Clara saying once before to focus on the centre of the forehead and repeat "I am a peaceful soul".

He did this for ten minutes, following which he rested his fingers gently on the piano keys.

With his eyes closed, he started to play. He wasn't thinking about what he was doing, rather feeling it. It was a safe, relaxed feeling, and playing the piano seemed to come naturally to him. When Damien opened his eyes, he was immersed in the golden light he'd seen at Jerry's. It was all around him as if hugging him. It was sparkling and felt like visible love.

This time Damien knew how to make it last. Just be! Be in the room, be one with the piano and his surroundings. It's the thoughts that take you away. It only takes one thought, such as I'm doing really well here, which leads to another I wish my friends could see me play and so on, and before you know it, you've drifted out of the sparkly love feeling and into your mind. Then, you lose your flow.

The more Damien played, the higher he felt. Thoughts did pop in his head but he recognised them quickly and let them go.

He could feel himself lifting, almost as if his body had disappeared. Then, he made a connection he'd never forget.

"John!"

"Damien, keep playing."

John was one of Clara's closest friends. He had been a photography mentor to Clara since she was 16. He used to say Clara was like the daughter he never had. John passed away last year. Clara had been receiving messages from him during her meditations recently. It seemed like he wanted to help them.

"The cats represent fear, Damien," John continued.

"Remember what I told you, that anger feeds off fear? When the cats are scared, they get angry and attack. The more fear they feel, the bigger and more dangerous they get. Damien, you have to help the cats. Find out what they're afraid of."

Damien took what John was saying on board with a surprisingly calm attitude.

"How, John? How do I find out what they're afraid of?"

"Be with them. Be kind, help them. The angel of peace will help you. She is up here with me. Her name is Archangel Muriel. To call upon her, you need to hold some flowers, face south, and softly call out Angel Muriel's name repeatedly. Call on her when you get frightened, Damien. Fear is catching. It triggers fear inside whoever is near. You have to be stronger than that. You have to make the light of your soul bigger and stronger than the fear around you. If you need help to feel strong, find the horse called Strength."

"Horse called Strength? Where, John?"

John's voice was fading. "Jeremy…"

"John?" Damien had lost his connection.

Completely oblivious of the fact that he was still playing the piano, Damien opened his eyes to the most beautiful sight he'd ever seen. The golden glow was brighter than ever and what looked like shooting stars were flying all around the room. It was like a glimpse of heaven. Damien continued to play the piano in total bliss. It was one of the most amazing experiences of his life.

Chapter 9
The Power of Faith

Melanie instantly fell in love with Purity, the stunning white owl. She couldn't wait to tell her mum about their day at the rescue centre. She was never going to believe they'd taken in a lion cub and a barn owl.

"Do you fancy a cuppa?" Brenda called to Melanie.

"Oh yes, please! Tea, please!"

Melanie was playing with Pride out on the grass in the sun. The lion cub seemed very bold. Melanie wondered where he was from and what brought him to Devizes.

Brenda joined them and sat in the shade, sipping her tea.

"What are we going to do with Pride and Purity?" Melanie asked, bracing herself for a response she may not want to hear.

"I honestly don't know, dear. Don't forget we are all about finding animals a good home. Pride and Purity are no exceptions. It may just be a little more tricky to find than with cats and dogs."

Brenda and Melanie smiled warmly at each other and realised they were both feeling the same.

Just as Melanie was about to dunk a biscuit in her tea, her phone rang, alarming her somewhat.

"You're so jumpy," Brenda laughed as Melanie fumbled

around at the beck and call of the shrill sounding phone.

"I was so relaxed! Stupid phone," Melanie replied, half-joking.

"Mum, slow down. I'm fine, Mum, what's the matter?" Pride came and sat right by Melanie as she took a deep breath. Her mum sounded panicked.

Brenda, trying not to earwig on Melanie's conversation but equally concerned, got up and put Pride in his enclosure. She went and fed the birds and checked in on Purity. When Melanie got off the phone, she was in a bit of a state.

"Mum says I have to go home," Melanie squawked, almost crying.

"She said there's a warning on the news about a pandemic of fear. People have been told to stay inside. She said to look out for black cats and that they're dangerous. I thought it was a joke but then Mum started crying!"

Brenda, looking wide-eyed and nervous, tried to be calm for Melanie.

"It's OK, don't panic. I'm sure whatever it is has been blown out of proportion by the news. It'll be fine. Trust me. We better get you home."

"But I don't want to go home. I want to stay here with you and the animals. We're in this together. I can't just leave you on your own if there's something scary out there. What about Pride and Purity? No one will know how to handle them properly."

Brenda didn't know what to say. Melanie had a strong will and equally strong ethical values. It's what she loved about her.

"OK, why don't we go for a walk, talk it through, and when we get back, I'll call your mum," Brenda said, already forgetting that the warning was to stay inside.

Melanie, looking relieved, pulled her hat down over her forehead and grabbed her cardigan. "OK. I'll just wash the cups. I'll meet you out the front."

"OK dear," Brenda replied, pulling the heavy front door open. As she stepped outside she caught her breath. It wasn't just the number of cats that shocked Brenda; it was the look in their eyes.

"What's up?" Melanie called from the kitchen.

Brenda was standing out the front of the rescue centre surrounded by black cats. She wasn't the sort to get easily scared, especially by animals. Bending down over the cats, she wondered why they all looked so afraid and tried to call one to her. All the cats had black eyes and stood close to one another as if for comfort.

Melanie emerged from inside and gasped.

"Brenda. Black cats! Mum said they're dangerous."

"They don't look dangerous. They look frightened."

A loud bang broke the conversation and made the pair jump. "What was that?" Melanie asked, anxiety building up inside her.

The cats cowered down, looking petrified now.

"The cats are getting bigger!" Melanie shrieked.

She was right. The cats seemed to be growing. They looked almost twice the size now and they weren't huddling up to each other for comfort anymore. They seemed to be turning on each other.

"Brenda, let's go in."

"Yes, OK. Come on in. Perhaps we should put the news on and call your mum, figure out what to do."

Brenda locked the door, leaving the cats hissing and

scratching each other.

"Brenda! Quick! Faith has escaped!"

"Whatever next," Brenda thought. The naughty white bunny had managed to dig his way out of his enclosure and was sitting next to Pride's enclosure.

This was the fourth time this had happened. Brenda had tried everything to keep him in, bits of wood over the grass, chicken wire on top of the already high fence. There was plenty of space in empty aviaries on concrete but Brenda wanted Faith to be on the grass. It seemed so unnatural to put a bunny in a concrete enclosure.

The last time Faith escaped, he was sitting next to the aviary. Purity was sitting on the other side of the railings, right next to the white rabbit. It was almost as if they were having a conversation.

Melanie sat down a couple of feet away from her favourite bunny, careful not to scare him.

"This is all so strange," Brenda said, shaking her head slowly.

The sweet white rabbit turned to Melanie and ran directly into her arms. Melanie caught her breath and scooped him up. The rabbit was standing on his back feet, reaching up towards Melanie's face. Melanie lifted him higher to look into Faith's eyes. The pair sat, eyes locked for a few seconds before the confident rabbit leaned forward and licked Melanie's nose.

Brenda and Melanie looked at each other.

"I think that's a message for us to have Faith," Brenda said, smiling.

Chapter 10
Losing Strength

Jeremy stood, too scared to move. It was the biggest snake he'd ever seen.

The snake stopped and looked at Jeremy for a few seconds before returning to what it was doing—eating his mum's flowers!

"I thought snakes ate mice," Jeremy said out loud, looking at the snake as if waiting for a response. "You're spectacular," he continued, suddenly feeling more curious than scared.

The snake moved towards Jeremy, still eating everything in sight.

Jeremy wondered what it would be like to touch a snake. He'd never been this close to one before. He sat a couple of feet away from the snake in the direction it was moving, hoping it wouldn't change course. The snake got closer, and Jeremy bravely held out his hand. The snake slithered up him wrapping itself around his arm as if it was a tree branch.

Jeremy felt excited and had an idea.

"You can be my fabulous new pet!"

The snake continued climbing up Jeremy's body, all the way to his head.

"That tickles," Jeremy said, giggling.

Jeremy was wearing his favourite wool beanie hat that his mum knitted him. It was blue with a red stripe and wasn't itchy like the others. The snake liked his hat too and had begun eating it, right off his head.

"Stop it, you naughty snake!" Jeremy shouted, almost as if it was completely normal to be wrestling his hat out of a snake's mouth.

"I'm going to name you Greedy!" He continued, already feeling annoyed with his new friend for putting a hole in his best hat.

Wondering how he would get Greedy past his mum, Jeremy stood up with the snake hanging around his neck and went looking for something to put him in. He went into the shed and found a linen potato sack and tried to usher the slithering snake into it. At first, he hadn't noticed the four black cats sitting near the shed door. It wasn't until Greedy started lurching towards them that he realised there were even more outside the shed. In fact, they were covering the lawn.

"Look! Cats! Lots!" Jeremy said, chatting away with the snake. "No, what are you doing? You can't eat cats, you terrible snake!"

Greedy was writhing around in an attempt to reach the cats, which were beginning to look frightened. As the snake broke free from Jeremy's grasp and chased one of the cats, Jeremy watched in horror as the others started growing at a phenomenal rate.

"Greedy. NO! You're making the cats get bigger!"

Jeremy chased Greedy through the army of black cats. He managed to catch the snake before any cats got eaten. He put Greedy into the sack and tied the top in a loose knot. The black cats closest to Jeremy were three times the size of a typical cat, and the rapid growth spurt seemed to spread through the other cats as if it was catching. The bigger the cats got, the more aggressive they appeared.

"The cats are fighting!" Jeremy said through the linen sack, keeping Greedy informed of what was going on.

Jeremy didn't seem too worried about the cats. He was more fascinated than scared. He walked towards the house, more concerned with how he would sneak past his mum with a thrashing sack than the fact that his garden was full of giant black cats fighting.

"You all right, love?" Jeremy's mum called from the sink, luckily not turning to greet him.

Jeremy walked quickly past, hiding the sack behind the wooden table that ran down the centre of the large country house kitchen.

"Dinner in ten," Jeremy's mum continued. She'd decided they would tell him over their meal about the warning she'd heard on the news. It was always a little difficult knowing how to approach these subjects with Jeremy because they never knew what reaction they'd get. Jeremy could be easily upset. And like the cats, when he was frightened, sometimes, he became angry.

"OK, Mum," Jeremy said.

Mrs Burgess always knew when Jeremy was up to something because he only said a few words and had a neutral persona! She chose not to play detective today. Jeremy managed to slip through the house to his bedroom.

"You stay here, you fabulous snake." Jeremy smiled at Greedy as he put the snake on his bed.

Jeremy was heading back down the stairs following the smell of cottage pie when he felt the urge to stop a moment.

He leaned against the wall by the window on the half landing. As he stopped, he began thinking about everything that had happened that day, and how much he already loved his new pet. He was smiling to himself and could feel the love inside him. It was like a gentle tug on his heart. Suddenly aware of every sensation inside him, Jeremy felt unusually rooted to the ground. He could hear the soft mutterings of his family chatting in the kitchen, his dog's wagging tail banging against the table leg, and the distant sound of the radio coming from his dad's office.

Jeremy felt surrounded by love. He realised the love he felt for his family and the love they brought him were what kept him going, and even if he struggled to show it sometimes, he was very grateful.

What he saw outside the window next brought him back to earth with a thump.

"MUM! STRENGTH IS RUNNING AWAY!" Jeremy screamed, panic erupting out of him.

The beautiful white horse was galloping faster than Jeremy had ever seen him move, and he was heading straight towards the closed gate.

Jeremy stayed, glued to the floor, watching out the window in horror. Strength leapt into the air, clearing the gate with ease.

"HE'S GONE!" Jeremy wailed, dissolving into tears.

Jeremy's mum came running towards him, while his sister darted out of the door to look for Strength. She wasn't expecting to be faced with a garden full of giant cats. She came straight back inside and slammed the door.

"Rob, please come down here," Jeremy's mum called up to his dad as loud as she could.

Jeremy lay down with his head in his mum's lap, sobbing. "We've lost Strength," he whimpered.

Chapter 11
The Premonition

Clara and Damien wandered slowly across the field not far from where they lived. The long grass tickled Clara's ankles. Since Damien's message from John to get close to the cats and see what they've been afraid of, Clara and Damien had been taking less notice of the warnings to stay indoors. It felt as if they had inside information and were one step ahead of the government.

"He said I could call upon the angel of peace when I get frightened, Mum. It's almost too much to comprehend."

"It's incredible, Damien, you have a gift. You have a particular purpose in this world. Don't put too much pressure on yourself; go with the flow. When you've learned and experienced everything you need to, you will carry out your purpose and you will feel amazing."

Damien was making sense of what his mum had said when out of nowhere, the biggest beautiful white horse they'd ever seen came galloping towards them. It was breathtaking like something out of a movie. It sped straight past them into the forest behind them.

"Mum, it looked frightened!"

The pair ran into the forest and watched the horse go from

a gallop to a trot and then stop. The horse turned around and stood looking at them almost as if it knew they were there to help.

Clara walked slowly towards the horse, whispering over her shoulder to Damien, "You wait here."

Luckily, the horse was wearing a harness, so Clara had something to hold.

"What are we going to do, Mum? And no, we can't take a horse home!"

It was a bit of an ongoing joke that Clara always wanted to rescue lost or injured animals and take them home. She'd followed a donkey and some goats down the road the other night. The animals were lost in the dark and Clara found herself wondering how she could get them home. And then there was the time they took Damien on holiday when he was little; there was a poorly sheep in a field, and she begged Damien's dad to help her pick up the sheep and put it in the boot of the car so she could make it better and it could live in the garden.

Lost animals seemed to be attracted to Clara, and she ended up with a garden of unwanted pets and adopted rabbits, and once, even a tortoise showed up on her doorstep. Someone found it and heard about all her animals and thought it must be hers.

"We could call the lads!"

"The firemen, you mean? You just want to sit on the nee-naw, don't you?"

When Damien was a toddler, sometimes he used to watch Clara go on a shout from the fire station. He used to say, "Mummy going in nee-naw now." She felt so proud watching Damien stand with her cousin in the fire station, waving her off as the pump flew out the station bay.

"OK, what about the police?"

"What about the animal rescue place your photography student works at?"

"Ah, Melanie! Yes, good idea! It'll mean walking the horse through town, though. What do you think?"

"I think it'll be fine, and if they can't help, we can call the police."

"Good plan!" Clara replied, grateful to have such a caring, smart son.

Clara and Damien led the horse out of the forest. The air was fresh and there was a strange orange tint to the sky. Clara started to reflect on recent events when she suddenly made an important connection.

"Oh!" Clara gasped. "Damien, do you remember that premonition dream I had about a year ago? The one where I asked for the shooting star?"

"The one about the new beginning? Yes, of course."

Damien's eyes widened. He'd just clicked. "You think it's linked to what's happening?"

Clara often had visitation dreams but this one was different. It was a warning, and it really scared Clara. The dream was a message that something terrible was coming, a tragedy. There was a strong sense of danger and Clara was petrified when she woke up. But then she got another message, "It's not the end of the world, it's a new beginning. You have to reach people, get them to believe, find faith."

Clara went straight downstairs, opened her patio doors, and said to the sky, "If this is a message I need to tell people, please send me a shooting star." No more than ten seconds later, the biggest shooting star Clara had ever seen shot through the sky right above her.

Shaken to the core, she ran upstairs and got an old piece of wood and began painting. But something else was controlling the brush.

Clara knew from that night that she was an important messenger and tried to help people find something to believe in, which was always a delicate balance to strike. Finding her faith had helped Clara to live a more meaningful, happy life, where things made sense but she didn't feel comfortable trying too hard to lead others in that direction, even though she knew it could help. It was so frustrating sometimes.

Her painting made so much sense now, though, and she knew she must try to lead whoever would listen towards awakening.

"It's the book, Damien! It's my chance to finally reach people!"

"Yes, Mum! Please do it! Write! And you could have a YouTube channel to show people your painting and all the great stuff you're working on."

Clara felt excited. She could write about everything in the book without having to dampen down her spiritual side.

"Good idea. Yes," Clara said assertively. She was seeing things clearly and a new energy had washed over her. "If I had a YouTube channel, I could really inspire people on there."

Damien was pleased to see Clara excited. "Yes!" he said, matching her enthusiasm.

"We're nearly there already!" Clara had been enjoying chatting with Damien so much that she barely noticed they'd walked all the way through town.

"Yes! And the horse seems pretty calm." Damien replied, sounding relieved.

Chapter 12
Friends Reunite

Melanie seemed so pleased to see Clara standing on the doorstep that she almost didn't notice that she had a horse in tow.

"Clara, hi!" She said with a lovely smile that caught Clara off guard.

"Hey, you!" Clara responded with a warm, grateful voice. It was so lovely to see Melanie's friendly face.

Melanie shot Damien a coy smile then looked directly at the horse, her expression changing to shock.

"We didn't know what else to do!"

"Brenda, you better come out here!" Melanie called.

Brenda came scurrying out, muttering something about owl food to herself.

"Oh, my goodness! It's young Jeremy's horse!"

"Jeremy? Jeremy Burgess? I didn't know he had a horse! Must be a new addition."

Clara used to work for Mrs Burgess, helping out with the pyjama business. Jeremy often came and chatted with Clara while she was sewing and they became friends. Clara invited him over a few times. She liked having him around; he was a breath of fresh air, always smiling and willing to help out.

Clara sensed that Jeremy enjoyed her busy upbeat lifestyle.

"Well, let's bring Strength around the back and find him a snack while we call the family, they must be worried..."

"What did you say?" Damien cut in.

"What, dear? Are you OK? You look like you've seen a ghost."

"You said Strength."

"Yes. That's the horse's name."

"A horse called Strength. Jeremy." A tingle ran down Damien's spine. He stood wide-eyed, staring at Brenda.

Clara nudged his arm as if to prompt him to pull himself together.

"It's all very odd," Brenda continued, oblivious to the black cats that had slipped into the centre while they'd been talking.

Strength was a stunning horse and true to his name; looking strong he had a mighty presence.

"We now have a lion called Pride, a rabbit called Faith, an owl called Purity, and a horse called Strength," Melanie blurted out, her cogs clearly turning.

"My friend's dog is called Love," Damien responded, instantly making the connection.

"Mum," he continued, "what are the original qualities of the soul again?"

"Love, truth, purity, joy, peace. Close. Very close." Clara replied, also trying to piece things together.

"And the cats represent fear."

"The cats represent fear?" Melanie and Brenda said in unison.

Damien didn't mean to say that part out loud.

Brenda and Melanie were staring at him, waiting for him

to give them a bit more.

What was he going to say now? They'll think he's crazy if he tells them about his conversation with John.

"Just a theory. Can I meet the other animals?" Damien asked, hoping he'd got away with it.

Pride looked much bigger already like he'd doubled in size almost overnight.

"A white lion? You have a white lion?"

"Wait until you see the others. They're all white!"

"White with gold eyes," Brenda added.

"What colour is your friends' dog?"

"White!" Damien exclaimed, catching eye contact with Melanie.

Melanie blushed and turned around.

"I'll go and get Faith. They all seem so tame. It's like they're trying to communicate sometimes, isn't it, Brenda?"

"Definitely. Something very odd is going on."

It was then that the four black cats wandered to where Damien was standing. Purity squawked an alarm call, and the cats cowered down, looking both frightened and hostile.

"How did they get in here? Brenda, I'm scared," Melanie said, holding Faith close to her chest and looking a little embarrassed.

"It's all right," Damien replied. He put a hand on Melanie's shoulder, and she blushed again.

"They're just frightened. We have to try and find out what they're afraid of. They grow as their fear grows."

"How do you know all this?" Brenda asked, comforted by the young man's confidence.

"It's a bit of a long story. Let's work together and see what else we can find out."

65

The four cats already looked bigger. They started hissing and clawing at the cage where Pride sat, seemingly unbothered.

Melanie screamed as one of them jumped towards Faith. Damien instantly stepped in, getting between Melanie and the cat.

"Perhaps we should put the rabbit back where it's safe," he said, leading Melanie towards the small animal section.

The cats were getting bigger and more aggressive now. Damien looked at his mum, not knowing what to do. The white horse came over to Damien and nudged his shoulder. Damien turned to the beautiful horse and looked straight into his golden eyes. It was mesmerising and reminded him of the golden glow around his piano.

"He's giving you strength," Clara whispered, trying not to break the connection between Damien and the horse. Damien held the horse's head between his hands and said a meaningful "thank you", then turned to one of the giant angry-looking cats and picked it up.

Chapter 13
Wedding Plans

Jeremy was sitting in the large living room, peering out of the window, still crying. He felt so hopeless.

"MUM!" He yelled, not knowing why he was calling her.

Mrs Burgess was there in seconds.

"Are you OK?"

"Where's Strength?" Jeremy asked desperately, without hope or expectation.

"Sweetheart, we're doing all we can. Please try not to worry."

Mrs Burgess could see Jeremy's emotions change.

"I'm not waiting. Strength needs me. I have to go," Jeremy's anger started to build up.

"You can't go out there, sweetheart, why don't we play a game while we are waiting to hear back from the police. I rang them over an hour ago, we might hear soon."

"You are not my boss!" Jeremy shouted.

His sister, Lucy had heard the commotion and joined Mrs Burgess to try and console Jeremy so things didn't escalate.

"Hey, Jez, do you still want to help me with the bunting?" Lucy asked in a sweet soft voice.

"NO!" Jeremy snarled.

"I know you're cross," Lucy said calmly, "you're cross because you're feeling scared, aren't you?"

Lucy was always good at diffusing a situation with Jeremy, who found it difficult to cope with his emotions. When she reminded him that it was fear underneath the anger, he softened, returning to the vulnerable lad who wanted to be held and comforted.

Jeremy dipped his head and stared at the floor, nodding. Mrs Burgess gave Lucy a grateful nod.

"Why don't you come and help me with that bunting?" Lucy said, hopefully. Jeremy didn't respond.

"Come on, mate, let's go cut some triangles. And we'll put your flash dance music on. It'll make time go faster and might even be fun."

Jeremy nodded again and followed his sister into the large dining room where the coloured fabrics lay immaculately across the large wooden table. There were pale blue, pale pink, pale green and white. Jeremy grabbed a pair of scissors and began snipping around the triangles Lucy had carefully sketched onto the fabric.

Lucy and Peter's wedding was just two weeks away. The ceremony was to be held in the local church, and the reception would be in the garden of the family home.

"Guess what?" Lucy said to Jeremy excitedly.

"What?" Jeremy said. He tried to look uninterested yet was secretly curious.

"Aunty Jean has finished the cake! It's beautiful! You want to see it?"

Jeremy couldn't hide the little smile creeping across his face. Lucy went over to the shelves next to the large stone fireplace and standing on tiptoes, reached up to the top shelf.

She carefully took hold of the large white square box and lifted it down. She placed the box on the table next to the bunting and lifted the lid.

"This is the bottom tier," she said with a smile.

The cake was iced to perfection with bright white icing as pure as snow. Running around the bottom was pink and white chequered ribbon and little white stars. On the top were delicate pink rosebuds surrounded by tiny white flowers and pale green leaves. It was stunning.

"Lucy! You are getting married and your cake is fabulous." Jeremy said looking at his big sister with a tear in his eye.

"Ahh, Jez, come here." Lucy gave Jeremy a big hug and shook his shoulder. "I love you, Jeremy. Everything is going to be all right, you know."

"Thank you. I love you too," Jeremy replied, feeling grateful.

Chapter 14
Lockdown

Melanie admired Damien's bravery as he held the enormous angry cat in his strong arms.

"We have to pacify them," Damien said softly.

Brenda looked increasingly concerned as the cat struggled and scratched, its claws getting dangerously close to Damien's eyes.

"It's OK. He knows what he's doing," Clara said with total faith in her son.

Damien kept speaking softly to the cat in a soothing voice, and soon enough, the angry cat calmed down and began to shrink. "What's that on the cat's leg?" Melanie asked, looking rather disgusted.

"A leach!" Brenda said in horror.

"A leach of attachment," Clara blurted, not knowing where her statement had come from.

Damien turned to Clara.

"That makes sense. A cat representing fear, a leech of attachment, what else could there be?"

"A goblin called jealousy?"

The voice came from the doorway. It was Steve, the policeman. Everyone turned at once.

"Sorry. I let myself in. Things are crazy out there. And the Burgess family have lost their horse. I guess the search is over." Steve said, looking at Strength.

"I was going to call them any minute," Brenda jumped in, looking a little embarrassed.

"A goblin called jealousy?" Damien said, not so subtly diverting the conversation.

Steve seemed to brace himself and paused, trying to figure out how to begin.

"This is going to sound a little odd, to put it lightly."

"It's OK. We're getting used to odd!" Brenda said, trying to keep a light atmosphere. She was very protective of young Melanie, who got frightened easily.

"I cannot believe I'm saying this!" Steve continued.

"There are goblins outside. Lots of them. They hide in the trees. They have one green eye, and they growl. A girl I passed earlier told me there's a rumour they are something to do with 'jealousy'. They're aggressive like the cats."

Melanie looked like she was going to pass out. Damien gently put the cat down and turned to Melanie. He put an arm around her and stood strong, propping her up.

"I'm afraid it gets worse. The leaches are multiplying rapidly and are sucking the life out of their hosts. People and animals are dying from those things."

Melanie let out a frightened cry.

"It's OK, it'll be OK." Damien squeezed her closer.

"That's why the cats are frightened. It's the leaches."

"You could be right," Steve nodded at Damien. Then came the next bombshell.

"The country is going into what they call a lockdown."

"What's that?" Brenda blurted, not letting him finish.

"Everyone is being asked to stay indoors. It's serious. It will be policed this time. There will be fines issued to those who go out. It's for everyone's safety. The more hosts the leaches find, the faster they multiply. We don't know how to kill them either. Nothing seems to be working so far. I'm so sorry to scare you all, but you must know how serious this is."

Damien turned to Clara, who didn't say a word. She was still trying to take it all in.

"Mum, it'll be OK. We all need to work together. We can stop this," Damien said confidently.

"Do you know something we don't?" asked Steve, looking hopeful.

"I'll put the kettle on," Brenda said, grasping onto any sense of normality.

"Sorry, will you excuse me, guys? I need to make a couple of phone calls."

Clara swiftly escaped the room, feeling overwhelmed and took herself somewhere quiet to phone two of her close friends, Susie and Nicole. Clara rented a house with Susie when she was 19. They had the best time living together. Even though they both worked at that time, it was like being on a constant holiday! They never stopped laughing and having fun. Clara loved reminiscing about the good old times with Susie.

Nicole was one of Clara's closest friends at school. They'd kept in touch after they left, and Clara used to visit Nicole when she went to uni. The pair had a similar sense of humour and always managed to find a reason to have a shandy! Nicole got married a couple of years ago and now had three young children. They hadn't caught up in ages and Clara missed their giggles but she knew one day when the boys were older, they'd make up for the lost time.

"Alright, Nic! How you doing mate?"

"Haia'?" Nic replied in her beautiful Welsh accent. "It's been a long time, it has. How ah ya Mush?"

"I'm all right, thank you; I just wanted to check in on you, what with everything going on."

"Ahh, to be honest, like, I cannot believe it, what's happening. It's crazy it is."

"Yeah. It's weird. This will go down in history!"

"No kiddin'. So, ya settled into the new gaff?"

"Yes, thanks, it's lovely being near the forest. I'm surrounded by trees. How's Will and the boys?"

"Ah, that's lush that is! Yeah, they're good, thanks Mush. Oh, hold on…No! Not in your mouth! Flipping lego, mate!"

"Haha! I remember lego! It gets everywhere!"

"Ahh, don't! I trod on a corner piece the other day so I did!"

The girls laughed and chatted a while. It was so nice to talk about something lighthearted.

"Ah, I better go, mate, I 'ad. Will popped out, I'm on my own with the kids."

"No worries, mate, just wanted to say hi. Stay safe."

Clara said goodbye and was about to phone Susie when Damien came in.

"Sorry, Mum, didn't want to disturb you but Steve hasn't got long. I think it would be good for you to know what's going on."

"OK, I'm coming," Clara replied accepting denial wasn't an option.

Chapter 15
A Dragon Called Wisdom

"You need your dragon."

Clara didn't doubt that Damien could figure things out and help with this mess but she knew he'd need all the help he could get.

"Wisdom!" Damien replied gratefully as Brenda returned with a second cup of tea.

Wisdom was Damien's 'ideal other'. A rainbow-coloured dragon he developed in his mind after having compassion-based therapy. His therapist told him about the three systems in the brain: the threat system, the drive system, and the soothing system. The threat system is there to keep us safe, and when it's triggered, we go into fight or flight mode. The drive system is our motivation, our drive. The soothing system is when we are at peace with ourselves and are feeling relaxed.

Our brains can get confused between what is and isn't a real threat. It gets triggered when we aren't in danger. Some people with anxiety can live almost entirely through their threat system. Damien's therapist, Lyndsay taught him to build up his soothing system by doing what relaxed him such as music, being out in nature and writing. This brings balance to the three systems and can physically shrink the amygdala, the threat part of the brain.

Damien developed a 'safe place' in his mind. His safe place was a beautiful garden with a bridge over a river and a rainbow-filled waterfall. He took himself around the garden in his imagination, then sat on the grass and waited for 'Wisdom', his dragon. If Damien had any problems, he would speak to Wisdom, who always gave him a compassionate, loving response because Wisdom was like a best friend.

Lindsay also taught Damien to recognise which system he used to respond to life and to swap systems when he wanted.

"Do you think it would work on the cats, Mum?"

"What are you two talking about?" Steve asked, looking intrigued.

"Compassion based therapy," Damien explained.

"You can swap systems when you're experiencing anxiety or fear, just by realising you're in your threat system and doing something that relaxes you such as playing music, bathing or stroking a pet. I wrote a 'soothing system list' and used to pick one each time I needed some inspiration to get back into my soothing place."

Clara had a 'lightbulb' look on her face, liking Damien's idea.

"That's genius, Damien!" She said thoughtfully. "How can we soothe the cats? Let's brainstorm some ideas."

"I'll get some paper," Brenda said, looking much less defeated.

"Do you mind me asking why you needed therapy?" Melanie asked Damien gently.

"Of course, I don't mind." Damien smiled at Melanie. "It was after a car accident. I had PTSD."

Melanie gave him a sympathetic look, and this time didn't shy away from his eye contact.

Brenda returned with some paper and a pen, pleased to see Melanie looking more relaxed.

"Stroking the cats might soothe them." Melanie got the list started.

"Food?" Damien added.

"Playing with the mouse toy, my cats love chasing that," Brenda said, sounding quite upbeat.

"Catnip!" Melanie shouted as you would in a quiz.

"Brilliant!" Clara said. "We can use these to calm the cats down while we figure out what's at the root of their fear."

"Isn't it the leaches?" Steve asked.

"Quite possibly. But with fear, it's not always the obvious thing. We'll start with the leaches, keeping an open mind."

"So, are we going to try and remove the leaches?" Damien asked, looking slightly nervous.

"I think so, yes. What do we all think? Calm the cats down, remove any leaches then see if their behaviour changes?"

"Sounds like a good plan to me," Melanie said, sounding positive.

"How are we going to get the leaches off?" Brenda asked.

Damien jumped out of his chair.

"What is it, sweet?" Clara asked in a concerned tone.

It was like a burst of wisdom hit Damien. "The leaches represent attachment, so we need to treat them as if they are attachment rather than leaches."

"Yes!" Clara said, beginning to understand. "It's like a war between…oh my life!"

"What, Mum?"

"It's like a war between evil and magic!"

"My book!" Damien and Clara stared at each other. The fact that Damien was writing a book about a war between good and evil seemed fundamental but also irrelevant. They chose not to explain it to the others.

"The evil is the negativity we get possessed by on earth; fear, jealousy, and attachment represented by the cats, the goblins, and the leaches," Damien explained.

"The good is the qualities of the soul; Faith, purity, pride, strength."

"The dog called Love!" Melanie added.

"Oh, no!" Damien's eyes widened.

"What?"

"Fear destroys Love. The cats were trying to kill Jason's dog. We need to warn him."

"Yeah, and we need to get Strength home somehow," Brenda added, conscious that Jeremy would be waiting.

"I don't want to worry you guys but you know what this means, don't you?" Clara said, bracing herself.

"So far, we've only met fear, attachment and jealousy. There are sure to be more. We need to be very careful and stay aware. Remember what Damien said, 'If you're feeling scared, swap systems.' If we end up taken over by our distress, we will be adding to the problem."

Brenda and Melanie both sat still, listening carefully and nodding.

"Let's do this!" Damien said, ready for war.

Chapter 16
Research, Plan, Action

With Strength and Jeremy reunited and Melanie and Brenda safely home, Clara and Damien headed back to their place.

"You grab the laptop and paper, and I'll stick the kettle on."

"OK, Mum, lounge, yeah?"

"Let's sit in here, it's nice and light," Clara replied, looking at the breakfast bar in the airy kitchen. She pulled a tall stool out and handed Damien a coffee.

"Let's Google 'attachment'," Damien replied assertively.

"The leeches, yes…if they represent attachment, how to heal it? Overcome it?" Clara said, searching for the right word.

Damien started laughing. "It says here, try couples therapy."

The pair laughed. "We are going to have to think outside the box here," Clara said, sipping her coffee.

"What if we think of attachment as being similar to fear?"

"Go on…"

"Well, why do people get attached? Because they're scared of losing something, right? So, in a way, attachment comes from a place of fear. Meaning, we can treat it in the same way by soothing it."

"Damien, you're sounding really wise. I'm so proud of you!"

Damien smiled, and then continued. "Distraction could be another good way to go with this. If you're feeling attached to something or someone, distracting yourself can be a huge relief, and prevent an unhealthy obsession from growing." Damien was thinking more about Lisa than leeches now. As he briefly reflected on the issues in their relationship, he realised he felt much stronger these days. He missed Lisa but had a different perspective since dealing with such a huge crisis. It was beginning to help him see the bigger picture. Damien's sense of purpose, new friends and connection to music was helping him to heal his broken heart.

"Yes! Now you're talking!" Clara said interrupting Damien's thoughts. "We need to give the leeches something else to feast on. If we try to pull them away with nothing to latch onto, they could get scared and grow aggressive like the cats."

"Yep. They'll need a new comfort."

"Like a hobby! A book to write!" Clara teased, sensing he was thinking of Lisa.

"Yeah, cheers, Mum! Mindreader!"

Damien had been a little possessive over Lisa. He'd learned a lot since the split. His mum told him about loving unconditionally. When you love from a place of purity, without attachment, you feel free, happy, and safe. Many relationships feel like this to start with, then gradually, attachment, jealousy, and anxiety can creep in. Damien was right. Attachment and jealousy come from a place of fear as much as anxiety does.

"If we could just cure all fear, all the bad stuff would go away!"

It felt like an impossible task to Clara.

"We're not alone, Mum," Damien reminded her, sensing she was feeling overwhelmed.

Damien and Clara began brainstorming ideas for calming the jealous goblins, containing the leaches, and soothing the energy of fear in the air.

"It could become a vicious cycle," Damien murmured, only semi-conscious he'd said it out loud. He felt his mum's eyes on him and continued.

"The fear could spread so quickly among people that the energy of fear resonating off everyone could, in turn, feed the pandemic." Damien realised something as he spoke.

"What the 'Law of attraction' DVD taught us about fear attracting more fear is the same as what Lyndsay said. One person's threat system automatically triggers that of other people. It spreads. We need to help the people just as much as we need to help the cats."

"Yes. I've been thinking about this. There are a lot of frightened people out there. I wondered about making a 'self-help sheet'; a sort of mental health toolbox. What do you think?"

"Great idea, Mum!"

"Why don't we ask Melanie to take that on? With Brenda and Melanie on board, we can get things done much faster. We could all brainstorm ideas for the information sheet, and Melanie could type it up. Then, we need to get it delivered to as many houses as possible."

"Yes. I think they'd like to be involved. It will give them a purpose and something positive to focus on. I'll go and call

Melanie now and organise a meet-up. How about tomorrow?" Damien was already strolling out of the room, dialling Melanie's number.

"Sure. Tomorrow is fine," Clara called after him, smiling to herself.

When Damien came back into the room, he wasn't prepared to see his mum lying on the kitchen floor, face down and unconscious.

"Mum!" He shouted, rushing to her side.

"MUM!" He gently shook Clara's shoulders but she didn't respond.

Chapter 17
Teamwork

The ambulance arrived much faster than Damien imagined. Clara was taken to the hospital, still unconscious, and Damien was advised to stay at home. It was a long evening worrying about Clara. Eventually, he went upstairs to bed and fell asleep still trying to figure out what had caused his mum to collapse.

"Mum was passed out on the floor after our phone call," he explained to Melanie and Brenda the next day.

"She's awake now. The doctor said she could come home later today if she's feeling strong enough."

"What happened?" Melanie and Brenda asked at the same time.

"I have no idea. I went into the lounge to call Melanie, and when I got back, she was lying there. She's been low lately. She perks up when there are people around or if she's helping people but I can tell by the tone of her voice and the look in her eyes that something's wrong. I think it's to do with her and Toby."

"Oh, poor Clara." Brenda sighed. "All she's ever wanted is her happy ever after, isn't it?"

Damien nodded and changed the subject. "So how did you

get here without getting caught? I didn't want to cancel our meeting. It's important to make progress."

"I rang Steve and told him we were coming over to you to work on a help sheet for fear to post out. He sounded impressed and said as long as we were comfortable taking the risk to get here, he would back us up if anyone stopped us. Melanie's mum has been amazing too. She's so proud of Melanie and said she trusts her judgment on this one. I think your mum is glad you have something positive to focus on." Brenda turned to Melanie who was already jotting ideas for the help sheet.

Melanie smiled at Brenda, and then eagerly began. "I thought we could write about the compassion-based therapy you were talking about the other day," she said to Damien directly.

"Yes. Good idea! And we can mention local therapists too. Mum's been seeing a hypnotherapist called Andy Keogh. He has a room in Corsham. We could put his contact details on there for those who want to get professional help."

"Great idea! Hopefully, people will be allowed to travel if it's to get help," Brenda added.

The three worked together, brainstorming ideas until Damien couldn't take the suspense any longer. "I'm calling the hospital," he said, walking out of the room.

Brenda and Melanie sat quietly, waiting for him to return when there was a knock on the door. Brenda got up to answer it.

Steve, the police officer, was standing on the doorstep with Jeremy beside him.

"Caught this young man running like there was no tomorrow. He insisted that he must see Clara. Can we come in?"

"Of course," Brenda started, and then remembered the situation. "Clara isn't here though, I'm afraid. She's been taken unwell and is in hospital. Damien is just on the phone with them now."

"Oh. What happened? Poor Clara. She is my friend. I will look after her at my house," Jeremy said, sounding panicked and eager to help.

"How kind of you, Jeremy." Brenda smiled. Just as she was wondering what to say next, Damien called out, holding the phone to his shoulder. "Mum's ready to come home, can we go and pick her up?"

"Of course, dear. I can drive," Brenda replied, happy to help.

"Yes, we'll be there soon to pick her up." Damien hung up the phone and thanked Brenda, almost oblivious to their new visitors.

"Hello, Damien. Don't worry, your mum is a spectacular strong lady with a fantastic heart." Jeremy smiled, reassuringly.

"Cheers, Jeremy. How you doing?"

"I want to tell your mum something, it's a secret," Jeremy continued, flashing Steve a sideways look.

Jeremy's Down syndrome meant that his perception of life was sometimes distorted. His yearning to fit in made him act more confident than he felt underneath, which occasionally got him into trouble.

"OK, Jeremy, do you want me to give her a message? Your secret will be safe with me."

"OK. I'll tell you in the kitchen." Jeremy walked into the kitchen and boldly closed the door, so no one could hear, then whispered in Damien's ear, "I've got a pet snake!"

"Oh wow! Mum loves snakes!"

"My snake has eaten nearly everything in my bedroom. I've named him Greedy!"

Damien laughed, then his face fell serious and he asked, "Where did you get your pet snake, Jeremy?"

"He was in my garden when the sky went orange."

Damien instantly made the connection. "Jeremy, I think we might need to tell Steve about your snake. In case it's connected to what's going on around here."

"No!" Jeremy yelled. "No one can take Greedy away. He's mine. He tidied my room, and I love him. I just need to hide him somewhere. Your mum will help me."

"OK, Jeremy, we'll keep it a secret and I'll speak to Mum when she is home, OK?"

"OK, Damien, you are a good man. You can be Greedy's bodyguard so that no one catches him."

"You know that Melanie and Brenda out there both work in the animal rescue place, don't you? What if Greedy went to stay there and you could visit him?" Damien suggested, knowing that visiting would be difficult in a lockdown but wanting a safe solution with minimum disappointment.

"Maybe…" Jeremy replied with a slightly suspicious look on his face.

"OK, I need to go and get Mum now." Damien opened the door to where Brenda, Steve and Melanie were standing.

"Can I stay here with Melanie?" Jeremy asked.

"It's fine by me," Melanie said shrugging and glancing in Steve's direction.

"Do I have p-permission, policeman Steve?" Jeremy pleaded with a playful smile on his face.

"Yes, OK, as long as your mum says it's OK. I'll call her now. She can pick you up from here later on, OK? Don't leave this house on your own please, Jeremy."

"I won't, Steve. You are wonderful."

Damien and Brenda made their way to the hospital and Steve headed back to the station, leaving Melanie and Jeremy standing in Clara's hallway.

Jeremy looked so happy to be trusted and felt excited to be part of something.

"Let's sit on the sofa, Melanie. We can talk about all sorts of things." He skipped over to Clara's sofa and made himself at home, pulling the blanket over his legs and snuggling into the cushions.

"Sure," Melanie replied, smiling and feeling grateful for such happy company.

Jeremy's smile was infectious. As Melanie walked over to the sofa, looking at his beaming grin, she felt her smile growing too.

"You look cosy," she said, feeling comforted by how relaxed Jeremy was.

"It's a spectacular house. My favourite colour is pink, and I like to listen to music and sing about it. I have responsibilities because I am an uncle and it's important to me like making new friends is important to me. My nephews are Aruth and Rupert of my brother, James. I also play football in Swindon town football club on Wednesday."

"Wow!" Melanie replied. "You have a lot going on."

Just as Melanie was about to sit down, Jeremy suddenly jumped up off the sofa in pure excitement and leapt across the room.

"A piano!" He sat at the stool of the piano and excitedly

turned to Melanie.

"Now I can make beautiful music for you."

"You can play the piano?"

"Of course. Anyone can play the piano. You just have to believe and be inside a dream."

"The world is your oyster, Jeremy," Melanie said, sincerely.

Chapter 18
Evil vs Magic

"I'll wait here, Damien," Brenda said as they pulled into a parking space. "Your mum will be so pleased to see you."

"OK, thank you. You sure you'll be OK? I could be a while."

"Yes, I have my crossword book, don't worry about me, take your time."

Damien crossed the car park and hurried into the main entrance.

"Hi. I've come to get my mum."

"Her name please?"

"Clara Allen."

"OK, she's in the Lavender ward. Go up to the third floor, turn right and head to the end of the corridor."

"Thank you." Damien hadn't noticed how many people there were around him until he went to the lift and saw all the people waiting. The corridor was full. He opted for the stairs. Shocked at how many people there were on the staircase, Damien also noticed most of them were wearing facemasks. What was happening?

Lavender ward was slightly less busy yet there seemed to be an air of tension. Damien had been in hospital many times before but it never usually felt so rushed and tense. He saw Clara instantly and rushed over.

"Mum. How are you? What happened?"

"Boy, am I glad to see you! Get me out of here!"

Clara suffered from strong claustrophobia around lots of people and sometimes felt trapped in busy environments. Hospitals were a real challenge for her.

"OK, Mum, but don't we need to wait for permission, for them to book you out or something?"

"I'm just waiting for the doctor to sign me off," Clara said, clearly feeling anxious.

"What happened, Mum?"

"It's fear, Damien. It completely took over me. You went to ring Melanie and I started overthinking about Toby and I. Things have been difficult lately and I thought it was over. I realise now I've been creating a vision of my future with him in it. So, the thought of losing the relationship meant the loss of a future I'd built up in my mind. It's a bit like fear and grief put together."

Damien nodded sympathetically; he knew that feeling so well.

"It hit me out of nowhere," Clara continued, "I couldn't breathe, and I passed out in the end. When I woke up, I was in the hospital and my whole body felt paralysed. They said I'd had a nervous breakdown. I'm sorry I didn't speak to you sooner. I didn't want you to be upset or worried."

"I knew something was up with you guys!"

"It wasn't just that. It was the house move, not knowing where we were going to be, the end of the lease coming up, the pandemic, worrying about you, it's probably been building up for a while and hit me all at once. I've had palpitations for a week or so now, I was just trying to ignore it."

"Fear again! All this fear. It's evil!"

"Yes! It definitely is. We need to get back to where we were. The quote from Frozen Two came into my head this morning, 'When you can't see a future, all you can do is the next right thing.' Remember when we sold the house we were excited about the mystery of what the future would bring? I need to find that feeling again, to trust in the magic of the unknown."

"Yes. Trust is the antidote to fear."

"Exactly." Clara looked exhausted but Damien could see a tiny glimmer of faith shining through.

"We also need to listen to the news just a little more!"

"Yeah, what's going on? I noticed people wearing masks and the corridors are packed."

"It's the pandemic. There are two types of evil; the fear which is hurting and weakening people and the deadly virus the leaches are spreading. The hospitals are becoming overrun. The NHS is struggling to cope. It's awful. The virus is contagious, that's why people are wearing masks."

Damien looked terrified.

"Try not to worry, buddy. We need to stay strong. Remember what I told you about stress and the immune system. It has a massive effect. Let's try and be calm. I'm going to focus on helping people in every way I can now."

"OK, Mum, we'll do this together. It'll be OK. I'm going to tell them I'm taking you home."

"Thanks! Will you grab a couple of face masks while you're there?"

"Sure!"

The drive back to Clara's was rather quiet. Brenda respected Clara's privacy. A simple squeeze of the arm and knowing look of sympathy was enough to tell Clara she was loved and cared for.

Clara unlocked the front door of her house and paused before opening it. She tilted her head and put her ear closer to the crack in the door. As she slowly opened the door, the sound got louder. It was the most beautiful piano she'd ever heard. The door seemed hard to open like she was pushing against a force coming from inside the house.

Suddenly, the door flung open as if the wind had changed direction and Clara, Brenda and Damien all gasped at the beauty.

Golden glitter was floating from the ceiling. The house was drenched in a warm golden glow as if the sun was shining out of every wall. White and yellow twinkling stars were shooting through the air amongst the glitter.

"Magic," whispered Clara.

Overwhelmed, Brenda stood, a single tear rolling down her cheek, and Damien held his mum's shoulders and whispered, "Piano Fingers!"

Chapter 19
Green-Eyed Goblins

Jeremy sat singing his heart out, bathed in a golden glow. Melanie was perfectly still on the sofa, mesmerised by the shooting stars, glitter, and sparkle all around them. The piano melody seemed to bounce off the walls, adding to the magic that filled the room.

Clara, Damien, and Brenda joined Melanie by the sofa, all of them now smiling ear to ear as they watched Jeremy, whose eyes were closed, completely lost in the moment. They listened as he sang his song.

Happy song here we are singing along with my best friend,

I care for music, and I feel I like to sing.

And maybe so happy times,

We are close to our heart, our life.

Jeremy was grinning and singing as if he was the only person in the world. As the song came to an end, Jeremy opened his eyes and jumped with surprise. He leapt off the stool waving his arms up and down as if orchestrating the glitter surrounding him.

"Fabulous magical music!" He danced around in circles in the glitter, hugging Melanie, Damien, Clara, and Brenda one by one.

"Clara, you are home in your magical golden room," he sang gleefully.

The whole room sparkled like the sunlight dancing on the sea on a bright summer's day. The light in the room felt as if it was pure love.

Brenda took Jeremy's hands and began dancing with him.

"This is the closest to a miracle I've ever been." She smiled, soaking up every moment.

Damien and Clara stood with their arms around each other, smiling and watching the magic unfold around them while Melanie sat, still grinning and slowly shaking her head in disbelief.

No one could have predicted things would change so quickly.

The glass from the window behind the piano flew into the room at a dangerous speed. Melanie screamed and pulled the blanket up to her chin.

The second smash came shortly after, and then the third until every window in the living room was an open mass of jagged, sharp edges and a cold draft.

Brenda fell to the floor and crawled behind the sofa, trying to shelter herself from the glass.

Clara and Damien ushered Jeremy and Melanie to join her.

"Everyone, stay down," Damien shouted.

As the love and sparkle in the room were polluted with clouds of fear, the golden glow began to fade.

"Come back, magic," Jeremy shouted to the last of the shooting stars as they faded away.

"It's fear," Clara called to Jeremy, equally desperate to

salvage some of the room's positive energy. "Everyone, focus on love and trust. This is a test. We must combat fear. We must not let it win."

Brenda closed her eyes and started repeating, "Love, trust, love, trust, love, trust."

Melanie and Jeremy joined in, while Clara and Damien watched as the spread of the dark clouds slowed down.

"It's working," Damien shouted, then joined the others, repeating "love and trust".

"Focus on your heart chakras," Clara said as she too joined in. The darkness of the clouds seemed to reverse. They were getting lighter.

"We're winning!" Jeremy said, standing up. "Go away, nasty fear. Come back, lovely magic," he sang, smiling again. "It's a game," he continued in a tone Clara didn't recognise. He looked straight at her as he spoke in an assertive yet calm voice. "Figure out how to win this game, and you will be living your purpose, helping people."

Clara looked at Jeremy in shock. The voice didn't belong to him, and she knew it was a message she must listen very carefully to. She stared at Jeremy, hoping for more clues.

"You need your helpers," he said, holding his straight face with an eerie look in his eye.

"The animals," Damien said, reaching out to touch Clara's arm.

Jeremy began singing cheerfully again, and Clara knew it was the end of the message. She turned to Damien.

"Jeremy is our key to getting the magic back. He's fearless."

"Yes. You're right. With his imagination, he can dream his way back into the golden light."

"We all can," Melanie added from behind the sofa.

The shattered glass was covering everything in the room. The cold wind blew into the house, bringing with it the question no one wanted to ask, except brave Jeremy. "What broke the window?"

As if in response to his question, seconds later, four goblins jumped through the broken window and sat on the piano, staring at Jeremy.

Chapter 20
From Fear to Faith

"Goblins of jealousy," Damien said quietly, not wanting to startle them.

"Jealous of our magic," Jeremy added, unaware of just how accurate he was.

"Remember, jealousy comes from a place of fear," Clara said, "Don't get angry with them, you will feed the negative energy."

"Compassion!" Melanie whispered to Damien while hugging Brenda, who sat shaking with her eyes closed.

The goblins peered around the room, each with one piercing green eye.

"Cats as well!" Jeremy said with a playful curiosity.

Two dark grey coloured cats wandered into the room from behind the piano, tiptoeing nervously across the broken glass.

Damien looked across at Melanie and Brenda, who were still huddling behind the sofa.

"We need the animals," he said.

"Yes, I know," Brenda said as if psyching herself up.

"We can go and get them," Melanie said bravely.

Brenda drove Melanie to the adoption centre, while

Damien and Clara stayed with Jeremy.

"My snake misses me," Jeremy exclaimed.

Damien suddenly remembered the conversation with Jeremy and filled Clara in on Jeremy's new pet.

"Jeremy, we need to get Greedy here," Clara said with urgency.

"This whole puzzle needs to have every piece put together to fix things."

"I would love to get Greedy!" Jeremy looked very excited.

"Come on, let's go now. Damien, you better come too, we don't know how dangerous those things are." Clara pointed towards the goblins that still sat on top of the piano. They seemed almost as if they were waiting for something.

"It's OK, Mum. I'll be fine. I'm not scared of them. I can clean up some of this glass."

Clara was reluctant to leave him but finally agreed.

"OK, but promise me you will shut yourself upstairs if they get aggressive. Brenda and Melanie should be back very soon."

"I'll be fine," Damien insisted.

Clara pulled on her trainers and ushered Jeremy out of the door, and as she left, she called out, "Focus on love and trust!"

Damien was about to start picking up the large pieces of glass off the floor when he had a sudden urge to play the piano. Not taking his eyes off the goblins, he bent down to pick up the stool. He tipped the glass off and put it back down as quietly as possible, not knowing what the goblins were capable of.

The goblins were sitting, huddled together, looking relatively harmless, so Damien carefully brushed more glass off the piano hood with his sleeve. He sat down and placed his fingers gently on the keys and, still face to face with the creatures of jealousy, found the courage to close his eyes.

After a couple of breaths, Damien focused on the weight of his body on the stool, the feel of the cool piano keys beneath his fingers, and the chilly breeze coming through the window. He was aware of the strange smell of the goblins. They smelt like the rubber toy trolls he used to have when he was little. Every troll had a different colour of hair, Damien loved collecting them.

He could hear cars in the distance and the mutterings of neighbours talking, perhaps about the disturbance. Damien was surprised no one had come by to see if everything was OK but he knew the level of fear at the moment prevented people from helping others.

Damien noticed his rising thoughts about the toy trolls and his neighbours and brought his attention back to the room, the seat he was sitting on, and the room's temperature. He focused on his soul, reminding himself of that eternal part of him that couldn't be harmed by any of this.

Damien's fingers began to play. He had gone beyond the mind. When the soul takes charge, the endless wisdom and creative flair are free to shine through.

Keeping his eyes closed, he played softly and effortlessly and could feel the tension in the air around him melt away. The air felt lighter, and he had that safe, homely feeling. He felt the familiar gentle tugging on his heart that reminded him of being excited, happy, or in love.

Damien could sense everything from the rattling breath of the goblins and the smell of the fresh air fused with a distant bonfire to the slight rumbling in his tummy. The unusual sounds coming from the cat sitting on the floor to his left made

Damien open his eyes. He was greeted with the golden sparkling magic they'd witnessed when Jeremy was playing, except this time there was the addition of the most beautiful rainbows all around him. It reminded him of his safe place and his dragon, and he smiled. The goblins huddled together fast asleep on the top of the piano, surrounded by glitter and rainbows. Shooting stars seemed to circle Damien, and there were shards of light coming from above as if shining from heaven.

Still effortlessly playing the piano, Damien turned his head to the left and did a double-take. The two dark grey cats had got lighter. They were rolling around like they were enjoying the warm sunshine, pawing each other playfully. What happened next brought Damien's piano playing to a halt. One by one, the cats' tails rolled up, like a bun in a lady's hair, and turned into a fluffy ball stuck on their bottoms. The cats' hind legs folded up, causing them to take a sitting position, and their hind feet were suddenly enormous! The cats' ears grew upwards and flopped down, hanging well below their faces. Damien watched in disbelief.

A cloud of glitter and rainbows surrounded the transforming cats, making them almost invisible. The glitter and white light swirled around them like a whirlwind, and then began to dissipate. Out of the sparkly white light jumped two of the most beautiful white rabbits Damien had ever seen.

"Fear turns to Faith," Damien said out loud, his eyes wide and mouth open.

The rabbits hopped around the room, playing, not at all bothered about the broken glass beneath their feet.

Damien heard Brenda's car pull up in the drive, and shortly after, Melanie pushed the front door open. She walked in, holding Faith in her arms. Surrounded by the golden glow, she looked beautiful.

Damien turned to face her. All he could say was, "When you're conscious, fear turns to faith."

Melanie stood frowning at Damien, unable to read the expression on his face.

"More rabbits!" Brenda said from behind Melanie. Brenda stood holding Purity, pointing towards two rabbits which were now running in and out of the floor-length curtains as if playing hide and seek. Brenda gazed all around her like a child at Disneyland watching the golden magic once again.

"The cats turned into rabbits when I played the piano," Damien managed, still stunned. "It's like the cats were prisoners of fear. When I was conscious, love and joy came back and broke the spell of fear. The cats are free now. Look how happy they are," he said, pointing at the rabbits playing around his feet.

Melanie and Brenda stood mesmerised by the magic around them, trying to comprehend what Damien was saying.

"Something pretty amazing happened to us, too," Melanie finally said. She was getting used to crazy mystical things happening daily!

Damien looked up, shaking his head as if to wake himself out of a daze.

"I can hear the animals. I can communicate with them."

"You're Doctor Dolittle!" Damien laughed.

"She's serious, Damien! She told me that Purity is here to help us purify our surroundings by cleansing the air to keep negative energies and entities away," Brenda informed Damien.

Damien's jaw dropped again. He stared at the beautiful white owl perched on Brenda's arm. Just as he made eye contact with the bird, it flew swiftly over to him, landing on his shoulder.

"Whoa!"

"See, he's trying to tell you!" Brenda smiled.

The owl gently tugged at Damien's ear with its beak.

"That tickles!" Damien smiled, shrugging his head away from the owl's beak.

Melanie stepped closer, observing the owl.

"He's asking you to take this feather for when you need it."

Damien turned his head to look at the owl, only half believing Melanie was the bird's translator.

The beautiful owl lifted its wing, spreading its pure white feathers out like a fan. With its strong beak, it tugged on one of the longest feathers until it came free. The bird turned to Damien with the feather in its beak and tilted its head towards him, inviting him to take the gift.

Chapter 21
Team Magic

"I'll distract your mum, you go and get Greedy!"

Jeremy was surprised at Clara's rebellious comment. He giggled and opened the car door. "I'll meet you back here, yeah?" Clara confirmed.

"I know the plan. Don't worry, Detective Clarabell, it'll all work out."

Clara laughed and relaxed a little.

"Your mum's in the greenhouse. Perfect...see you in a min."

Clara darted towards Mrs Burgess, suddenly looking forward to seeing what veg she was growing.

"Hello, Clara, how nice to see you."

"Hey! Great tomatoes, are they gardeners' delight?"

"As always!"

Clara made herself at home and began pinching side shoots off the tomato plants.

"How's the allotment going? I heard you did a big painting for them again this year. Lucy saw it online. She was very impressed."

"Ah, thank you! Yes, I enjoyed doing that! I haven't been up there quite as much this year but it's looking good. I had some corn on the cob the other day. The badgers left me just enough."

Mrs Burgess laughed. "Those pesky badgers!"

"I find it quite funny!" Clara smiled. "People get so cross at the allotment with the wildlife taking their veg. I say a prayer that there'll be enough for me and there always is. After all, the wildlife has shared the planet with us and has to put up with us destroying the place." Clara was so passionate about the subject. She found it hard not to get on her soapbox.

"You still fighting for a chemical-free allotment?" Mrs Burgess asked, detecting Clara's determination.

"Yep! One day, it will be completely organic up there if I get my way."

Clara never used pesticides or chemicals on her allotment. The earth was already so depleted of nutrients through killing the soil with chemicals. She had tried to convert others at the allotment to a more organic approach but was struggling. "We all need to do our bit to help the planet," she continued.

"I completely agree," Mrs Burgess replied, carefully removing a snail from underneath her grow bag.

"What brings you here today, anyway? It's been a long time. Scary world these days, isn't it?"

"Yes, it is. It's bizarre. I just brought Jeremy back. He wanted to grab something from his bedroom," Clara replied, not lying.

"Ah, it's nice of you to look out for him," Mrs Burgess said warmly.

Clara looked over her shoulder and saw Jeremy at the car with a sack in his hand. He lifted the boot lid and looked across at Clara, nodding his head in the direction of the exit.

"Ah, well, better get going! Lovely to see you!" Clara

said, trying not to leave too abruptly.

"OK, sure, Jeremy coming with you then?"

"Yes, he can stay for lunch."

Mrs Burgess turned to thank Clara who was already halfway back to the car.

"Bye," she called, waving after her.

"See you soon," Clara called cheerfully.

Clara was pulling out of the long driveway when she suddenly slammed on the brakes.

"Oh, my life! We're going to need Strength."

"Good thinking, Batman!" Jeremy replied as if it really was all a game. "He's in the field up the road!"

"Oh, thank goodness!" Clara replied, thankful she wouldn't have to return to the house and explain this one.

She pulled up in the passing place next to the field where Strength was grazing.

"You definitely know how to get to mine, yeah?"

"Yeah, sure!" Jeremy cheered, jumping over the gate.

Back at Clara's, Brenda led the fully grown white lion out of the car to the house.

"This is something else," Clara muttered to herself as she stopped a moment to take it all in.

Brenda caught sight of Clara pulling up and stopped to wait. The beautiful lion sat quietly by her side.

"Pride is massive!" Clara exclaimed as she got out of the car.

"I am so in love with this lion!" Brenda replied, unable to resist stroking its head every five minutes.

The lion nuzzled its head into Brenda's hand and nudged closer to her leg.

"That's amazing!" Clara said, feeling a little envious of

such an encounter.

As if reading her envy, Pride wandered over to Clara and rubbed around her legs. Clara could feel herself grinning, and she honoured the moment with silent gratitude. "Let's go inside," Brenda said, suddenly aware of the growing number of grey cats in the front garden.

"Oh, where's Jeremy?" She added.

"He's bringing Strength! I have Greedy in the boot."

"Oh my! Where are you going to put a horse?"

Clara smiled, quietly excited at the idea of Jeremy bringing the horse home.

"The back garden!"

"Brilliant!" Brenda laughed. "Just brilliant!"

Clara gently lifted the sack out of the boot, and the pair were making their way inside when Jeremy called out from behind them.

"Clara, wait for me!"

"Wow! That was quick!"

"Strength is super fast!" Jeremy said, grinning.

"Let's get him around the back. He'll be safe there." Jeremy helped Clara make some space for the horse to safely wander around the garden before meeting the others indoors.

"I could get used to this," Clara said, smiling at the golden glittery glow.

Brenda, Damien, and Melanie were all in the living room, sweeping up the last of the smashed glass. Purity perched on the sofa's arm, Faith ran around with the other bunnies, and Pride was sat boldly by the piano as if keeping watch over the sleeping goblins.

"Hello, team magic," Jeremy shouted from the kitchen. As he turned into the living room, he spotted Pride and Purity and jumped. "A lion! And an owl!"

"Jeremy, meet the crew!" Melanie smiled.

Jeremy got acquainted with Purity, while Clara watched as the goblins began to wake up. Pride watched as they stirred. On waking up, they saw Pride straight away. To Clara's surprise, they didn't get scared or angry. Instead, they all crept over the top of the piano to the big gentle cat. Pride placed his huge front paws on top of the piano. Standing upright, he was now facing the goblins. One of the goblins put its nose directly onto the lion's. The others sniffed his face, and he began licking them all in turn. The goblins nuzzled into the lion's thick fur, and two of them jumped onto his back. Pride seemed to be mothering the goblins.

"They're changing colour," Damien said from behind Clara.

He was right. The more the lion soothed the goblins, the more they seemed to change. Their green eyes turned pink, and their brown nobbly bodies slowly became smooth and turned to a pale-yellow colour. Suddenly, sparkling light and glitter surrounded Pride and the goblins. It swirled around them gracefully.

"A tornado!" Jeremy shrieked at Damien.

"It's OK, Jeremy, this is good. It's the magic doing its thing."

The whirlwind began to slow down a little, and out of the top jumped three baby lions. They ran to Pride, who lay on the floor, allowing the three babies to snuggle into her coat.

Everyone stood watching in amazement.

Damien spoke first. "I get it. When you soothe jealousy, you can turn it into Pride."

"Wow!" Melanie said, completely inspired.

"Amazing!" Clara added.

Jeremy went over and stroked the lion cubs. "Don't worry," he said, "I won't let Greedy eat you!"

Clara felt sudden panic and ran into the kitchen where she'd left the hessian sack with the snake in.

The sack was empty.

Chapter 22
Time Is Running Out

Clara had been on the phone with Toby for over an hour now. With Greedy safely back and in an old fish tank Damien found in the shed, the windows boarded up, and the animals looking settled, Damien had convinced Brenda it was time to call it a night. Brenda took Melanie and Jeremy home and told Damien they'd all see him in the morning.

It was after 11 pm when Clara came downstairs. She wasn't looking particularly upbeat.

"You all right, Mum?"

"You know…" Clara shrugged. Damien knew by her response that things weren't great.

"You guys were getting on so well before," Damien offered, wondering if she wanted to talk about it.

"Yeah, I know. Oh well. Toby has got stuff going on, looking for work and all that."

Damien trod very carefully on the subject and asked nervously, "Is he staying put at his place then?"

"Yep! And that's fine! Wasn't meant to be!"

"Everything happens for a reason, eh?"

"Exactly! I like what Vince said the other day, 'The best dreams are the ones we don't know we're going to get.'" Clara was so grateful for all her friends. They'd been there through thick and thin. "I'm kind of OK with going our separate ways now; it just took some adjusting to. I have so much to get on with." Clara diverted the conversation, conscious to focus on the positives. "My poetry book needs finishing, and I want to get on with the life coaching and my chemical-free cleaning product line I've been thinking about."

"Ahh, the essential oils products??"

"That's the one! I'm going to work on that soon. I have a feeling I'm going to be too busy to worry about it all."

"Glad to hear it, Mum, remember the message on the earrings Dan and Jayne got you."

"She flies with her own wings." Clara smiled. Those earrings had become a little source of strength for Clara.

"Everyone went home, then? Did you find Greedy?"

"Yes! He's in the old fish tank! All the animals seem pretty settled. Mum, do you think I'll end up being a decent piano player?"

"I think you're going to be amazing. But don't compare yourself to other musicians. The only thing you should compare is how you feel before and after playing. Instead of judging your music by how good you deem it to sound, become more conscious of how it makes you feel."

"Thanks, Mum," Damien said, realising he'd already fallen into the judgment trap.

"There's a thing called 'artist abuse'," Clara said, her enthusiasm increasing as she recalled, "That book, The artists way explains it. It's excellent. Think of your inner artist as a child that needs to be looked after and nourished, not criticised."

"Wow!" Damien replied, looking at things in a whole new

way.

"We better hit the sack soon," Clara said, looking at the oversized clock on the kitchen wall.

"Yeah, OK. So…what's the plan tomorrow?"

"We figure out how to stop this pandemic and save the world?"

"Good idea!" Damien said, pleased to hear Clara joking around again.

"Do you think the more faith people have, the more rabbits will appear?"

"Maybe," Clara said, picking up the white feather off the worktop.

"Purity gave me that feather! Melanie can hear the animal's thoughts." Damien realised there was so much to tell Clara. "Purity is here to purify the air of negative energy, and he gave me this feather to use when I need it. I have no idea what to do with it."

"Smudging!" Clara said, her eyes growing wider. Damien had heard Clara talk about smudging before.

"That thing you do when you burn sage?"

"Yes!" Clara giggled. Damien always laughed at Clara when she went around the house with a smudge stick.

"I wonder what we're going to do with Greedy," Clara said thoughtfully.

"It'll make sense when it's meant to. Just like the next chapter of our house adventure," Damien said, sounding very wise indeed.

"You're perfect for me!" Clara said, giving him a playful punch on the arm.

"I'll lock up," Damien said, walking to the back door. As he went past the fish tank where Greedy was coiled up, he noticed something moving on the tank's lid. He bent closer and saw that it was a tiny pink spider. It wasn't much bigger than a money spider but was such a bright pink that it glowed.

"Mum, look at this!" He called out.

They stared at the spider, then at each other.

"As you said, it'll all make sense!" Clara said, laughing. They left the spider where it was and went up to bed.

Clara fell into a deep sleep and dreamed of an old man with a white beard and a shaky jaw. He had a long stick and wore a silver robe. He said his name was Time. He told Clara that time was running out. Fear was spreading fast. In the dream, he handed Clara a silver robe and said, "When the demons try to possess you, if you wear this, they will bounce right off you and weaken."

Clara woke up the next morning and screamed.

Chapter 23
The Silver Robe

Damien was downstairs, admiring the slightly bigger pink spider when he heard his mum scream. He ran upstairs.

"Mum?" He burst into her room and was blinded by the light from the window, bouncing off something shiny on the bed covering her.

"It's heavy!" Clara said, lifting a corner of the mass of silver that lay across the bed.

Damien grabbed a corner and lifted it high, allowing the length of it to drop to the floor.

"No way!"

"It looks like something off a movie, Mum." Damien spun the silver robe to admire it from every angle. It was stunning. It was like tiny silver metal plates all put together. It had a hood with long tassels hanging from it.

Clara told Damien about the dream. Damien looked confused and concerned.

"When I had the breakdown, I had the worst nightmare I've ever had," Clara explained, "I knew when I woke up that it was demonic. I physically couldn't move. It was like I was paralysed and I was shaking all over. It was as if a dark entity was trying to get inside me. I was petrified for days and have slept with the light on since."

"Why didn't you tell me?"

"I didn't want to freak you out. Toby and I watched The Conjuring 2 a few days after the dream."

"You don't do horror movies!"

"I know. The film is based on a true story and confirmed my suspicion about my dream."

"Now you are freaking me out."

"Just like when you're happy and angels can reach you, when you're in a dark place of fear, you are closer to the dark side of spirit. The negative entities feed off your fear and do everything they can to keep you scared so that these entities can grow stronger. I figured all this out watching that movie."

"Now, the cloak makes sense!" Damien said, holding it up even higher.

"I think the man in the dream who calls himself Time is John. I think he's been with us the whole time. He's guiding and protecting us."

"Definitely agree there!" Damien replied, remembering his special connection with their old friend. Clara didn't respond. It was all so surreal. "Shall I make us a special coffee?" Damien asked, hoping Clara's expression would change. She looked like a zombie staring into the corner.

"That sounds lovely, thank you!"

Damien went down the spiral staircase, past the sleeping white lion at the bottom, into the kitchen and put the kettle on. He walked over to the fish tank to look for the spider. It was still there, and it was even bigger now, about the size of a 20 pence piece. It glowed brightly and was pink and had a diamond in the middle of its back. It looked like one of those beautiful glass animals his nan used to keep in the cabinet above the neglected fireplace.

Clara came downstairs, and Damien showed her the spider.

"It's beautiful. So perfect!" Clara said, completely taken in by the tiny creature. "It's like something out of a fairytale," she continued.

Damien laughed and did a funny impression of Clara in a fairytale. He was always playfully ribbing her about being in a dreamland.

"When this is all over, I'm looking forward to going to the forest to write together," Clara said, "It seems like ages."

The house that Clara and Damien were renting was right next to a huge forest. It was perfect for writing, exploring and quad bike adventures.

"Sounds good to me," Damien replied, pouring the coffee.

The sound of the door startled Clara which made Damien laugh again. "I'll get it."

"You're bright and early!" Clara said to Melanie as she grabbed another cup.

"Yes. I hope that's OK. Brenda dropped me off. She's going to get Jeremy."

"Dream team!" Damien winked at Melanie with a flirty way about him.

"Hey, check out this spider," he continued, waving Melanie over to the fish tank, "it's been sat here all night."

"The fairytale spider," Clara said playfully.

"It's about the conscience," Melanie said, moving her head as close to the spider a possible without touching it. "It's the spider of conscience," she repeated, "he's sent to help the snake focus on gratitude, not lack."

"You're amazing," Damien said directly to Melanie.

Melanie smiled, then continued, "Open the lid. The spider needs to get close to Greedy to help."

Damien opened the fish tank's lid, and they all watched the spider crawl into the tank and sit on Greedy's head.

"When Greedy becomes grateful, he'll be able to help us with our mission. He will become one of the team, a positive influence."

"OK, so we will have gratitude with us, purity…"

Clara started listing the animals, trying to keep up with everything that was happening.

"Strength," reminded Damien.

Pride, the lion, came and sat next to Damien as if to include himself in the conversation. "Pride!" He laughed.

"Your friend's dog called Love," Melanie added.

"Yes," Damien said, reaching for his phone he sent a quick text: "All right, Jase, can you come around with your dog? I'll explain later! Kettle's on, mate."

There was another knock on the door. Purity let out a squark and flew over to the door and landed on the handle as if trying to open it.

Melanie and Clara giggled at each other, and Damien scooped the owl up and put him on his shoulder before opening the door.

Jeremy and Brenda walked straight in, and Brenda handed Damien a box of shortbread.

"Can't have us eating all your biscuits, can we?" She smiled.

Damien took the box and thanked her before pulling up a couple of chairs.

"Right," he said assertively, "we need a bit of a plan here."

Melanie reached for her bag and took out a pile of written

papers.

"I've finished the self-help sheet and have delivered 500 door to door. My postman took a load too."

"Amazing! Well done! The aim is to reduce the fear. This should help massively. The leeches are a bit like the demons. They need fear to feed on, so they attach themselves to the cats and frightened people."

"Wow! Where did that come from?"

"I have no idea, Mum!" Damien admitted. "Makes perfect sense, though!"

"Yes, it does! So, we stop the pandemic from spreading by stopping the fear."

"Exactly. Remember, jealousy, aggression, greed, and attachment, are all rooted in fear. We need to show compassion to everything. Even the scariest horrible-looking things we come across. Don't think of this as a war, think of it as a rescue mission of all living things."

"It's pretty scary out there," Brenda admitted, "there are vicious cats and goblins everywhere, clouds of fog, and the sky is so dark."

"Shops are boarded up, and there's no one around," Melanie added.

Clara nodded. "I know it's scary. Try to remember, fear is created by us but spirit will always guide us from a place of love, so let them lead the way."

"Music!" Jeremy piped up. "We need magical music."

"He's right," Damien nodded. "Music is one of our greatest powers. Text everyone you know, telling them to play their favourite songs."

"Daniel and Ross could meet us with their guitars," Damien suggested.

"Yes! We need a base, though. It should be here. We need a place that's safe to come back to and recharge our energies. We could get Daniel and Ross to come here."

"Good idea," Damien said, picking up his phone again, he texted his uncles.

"Mum, you need to make sure you wear that robe. Out of everyone, you're most in touch with spirits, and you're vulnerable at the moment. You need protection."

"Robe?" Melanie asked

"Long story!" Clara said, dashing upstairs to grab it.

Chapter 24
Fresh Start

"New month, new start," Clara declared positively as she bounced back down the stairs holding the silver robe.

"That's the spirit." Brenda smiled.

When she got back to the kitchen, Damien was holding some flowers he'd picked from the garden.

"This is no time for picking flowers, mate!" Clara laughed, which soon gave way to a questioning look.

"Haha, Mum! They're to call upon the angel of peace. Remember what John showed me."

"Oh, yes! Good thinking! We're going to need her. Ahh, when I saw the flowers I thought you were off to see Lisa."

Clara's mind-reading abilities never ceased to amaze Damien. He had been thinking of Lisa amongst the chaos, now that he had found his purpose of helping people, he felt like a completely different person. He was ready to keep fear at bay and show Lisa the love she deserved. In coming together with his mum again, he had been reminded of the positive, philosophical way of looking at things that Clara had always shown him and he had new faith in himself and his future.

Clara was putting her robe on just as Jason let himself in through the front door. He had his dog by his side and his guitar on his back.

"All right, Damo," he called, not able to stop staring at Clara's new attire.

"This may all look a little strange, Jason but there's not much time to explain."

"It's all good," Jason said, not knowing where to look next.

Pride wandered over to Jason and he froze.

"It's OK, mate. This is Pride. He's a kitten, really!"

The beautiful white lion jumped up at Jason, nearly knocking him over. He placed his two huge paws on Jason's shoulders and licked his face.

"Whoa!"

Next, the lion walked behind Jason and started pawing at the guitar on his back.

"He wants you to play," Clara said.

"How did you know to bring your guitar, mate?"

"I didn't. I just thought I'd bring it in case you had time to chill. Clearly not, eh!" Jason said, laughing.

"We need you, Jason," Clara said, looking Jason in the eye. "We need you to play!"

"OK...is this to do with what's going on outside? Man, have you seen it out there?"

"It's everything to do with it. I'll explain it all later, mate. Can I borrow your dog?"

"Erm, Mum will kill me if anything happens to Love. She's still scared from before."

"Love is weak from fear," Melanie jumped in. "She needs Strength."

Jeremy, who was unusually quiet, perked up at the mention of his horse.

"I'll take Love to see Strength," he said, taking the lead off Jason and leaving him no choice.

"Don't worry, Jason. Trust me. We will take good care of Love. She's just been taken over by all the fear around."

Jeremy led the sweet dog out to the garden, and Strength immediately walked up to the dog and knelt beside her. The dog seemed to know exactly what was going on and jumped onto the horses back. Strength stood back up and bent around to the dog. He shook his head as if to get Love's attention and made eye contact with the little dog. The dog seemed to look deep into the horse's eyes, and after a few seconds, let out a little woof. She suddenly jumped off the horseback, wagging her tail and nudged the horse's leg as if to thank him.

Jeremy brought Love back. "What's my job?" he asked Clara.

"I need you to play the piano for us, Jeremy, and be in charge of Strength. We will need him if things get tough."

Clara took the boards off the windows so that the sound of music would flow out of the house.

"Yes, Miss Clarabell," Jeremy replied, and then turned to the glowing fish tank. "Greedy has turned golden!" He exclaimed, peering into the tank.

"We have ourselves some gratitude," Damien said with his thumb up.

"We'll explain later, Jeremy," Clara said before he could ask.

Clara couldn't help but notice that since Jeremy had been involved with helping them, his true caring nature was shining through. He finally had a real sense of purpose. Coupled with his raw sense of bravery in the face of danger, this meant he had become a great team player.

Damien took the golden snake and laid it across his shoulders.

"Brenda, can you stick with Melanie?"

"Of course."

"We need to stay in pairs, at least. No one goes anywhere alone. If we can all stay together, then all the better."

"Where do we start?" Melanie asked.

"Damien and I will take Gratitude…"

"Don't you mean Greedy?" Jeremy interrupted, sounding a little confused.

"Sorry, Jeremy, yes, I mean Greedy, but he's turned into Gratitude now, see, he's not eating everything in sight."

Jeremy didn't reply. He was thinking about his family. He realised that he was so blessed with love in his life. He had grown up a lot in the past few days and felt grateful to be trusted. He showed his friends a new level of respect and felt determined to show more love to his family from now on.

"We will take the snake and Pride and visit as many people as we can. We will deal with the goblins along the way."

"Mum, doesn't it make more sense if two of us deal with the goblins and cats and the other two visit people?"

"Mmm. Yes, you're right. OK, are you two happy to visit people and help them with their fear?" Clara asked Melanie and Brenda.

"Yes! We will take Faith and Gratitude."

"Good call! And we will take Love and Pride to deal with the cats and goblins."

"What about Purity?" Melanie asked.

The large bird flew across to Melanie and landed on her shoulder, rubbing its beak across her ear.

"Got your answer?" Damien smiled.

"He's going to follow wherever he's needed," Melanie replied.

Darkness loomed from the sky above their heads like a dead weight. There were angry fighting cats and goblins everywhere and patches of fog hiding pockets of negative energy.

Clara felt glad of her silver robe and pulled it tightly around her.

Damien was calling on Archangel Muriel when a white light shone down through the dark sky. A wisp of white smoke blew around them, and they knew they weren't facing this alone.

Before Clara could say anything, a dark cloud enveloped her, sucking her towards the dark sky. Being dragged along, she was heading straight for the angry cats and goblins, which looked like they were waiting to attack. Clara did everything she could to get out of the cloud but the force was too strong. She screamed.

Damien tried to jump into the cloud to help Clara but bounced off it. The fear wanted Clara for itself.

"Mum, focus on love and trust. You can do this." Damien took the white feather from his pocket and said a prayer while waving the feather through the air.

Clara began repeating "love, trust, love, trust" and imagined a white light of protection surrounding her.

Pride suddenly leapt from the driveway and made his way over to the first group of goblins, licking and gently playing with them. The golden glow began to rise around their feet.

Before long, the goblins had transformed into beautiful white lion cubs, which began running around in every direction towards the other goblins. The dark cloud lifted and Clara was able to run to where the others were standing.

"Start playing," Clara called to Jeremy and Jason inside the house.

"Perfect timing!" Damien shouted as he saw Daniel and Ross making their way towards them.

"This is mental!" Ross said, looking in every direction.

Clara caught her breath and calmed her panic by acting as if nothing had happened.

"Thanks for coming, guys. Jeremy and Jason are inside. Do you fancy a jam session?"

Daniel and Ross thought Clara was joking.

"Seriously, we need you to play! You'll see!"

"Never a bad time for a bit of Satriani!" Ross said to Daniel smiling.

The pair went into the house, plugged in their amps, and began blasting out one of their favourite tracks Circles.

Melanie and Brenda were already making their way to people's houses, and Damien could see her handing someone the white bunny through a window. He watched as the person took the rabbit and shone. A yellow light came from inside the house. Then, they handed the rabbit back to Melanie.

"She's literally giving them Faith!" Damien said, amazed by the perfection. As he watched Melanie take her new role, he was amazed at how much more confident she seemed now. "She'd make a good paramedic," he mumbled to himself.

As the music flowed out of Clara's house, so did the magical golden light. Sparkle and glitter floated after them down the road as they walked into clouds of darkness. Love, the dog was approaching the cats one by one and healing them. The more Love ran about to meet the cats, the more Fear turned to Faith, and there were soon more rabbits than cats.

As the swirls of golden light surrounded the frightened, aggressive cats and transformed them into happy, playful rabbits, the leeches attached to them turned into beautiful rainbows and disappeared.

The white wisps of light from the angel of peace swirled around, fusing the dark clouds with a little light. The golden glow coming from Clara's house began to spread everywhere, bringing with it a wonderful feeling of hope and safety.

People began to come out of their houses and dance in the golden glitter. Others stood listening to the music, and some even brought their own instruments and joined in.

Daniel, Ross, and Jason all came outside and played guitar to everyone around. Jeremy sat proudly at the piano inside and joined in with perfect timing.

Strength somehow made his way to the front of the house and was wandering around, spreading a sense of power. Jason's dog helped heal the fear with love, and soon enough, people regained faith.

Purity flew from house to house, cleansing the atmosphere and helping send the last of the negative energy away. The beautiful owl seemed to get bigger and bigger as it flew through the magical golden light. Soon enough, it was enormous and flew straight towards Melanie at great speed. Melanie stood, smiling up at the stunning bird as if she knew exactly what was going to happen next. The bird neared the ground and slowed, gliding within reach. Melanie ran alongside it before suddenly leaping onto the birds back.

Purity soared back up gracefully carrying his new companion into the sky.

The remaining clouds of black smoke exploded into the biggest most beautiful fireworks Clara had ever seen. She turned around and watched in amazement. Feeling overwhelmed, she started to cry. Damien put his arm around her and whispered in her ear, "We did it, Mum!"

Clara held his hand tightly. "For now," she said, "I want this magic to spread to the rest of the world." Clara realised just how important love and faith were to healing the people and the damaged earth. As she watched the beautiful animals and people working together and saw those she loved smiling again, she just knew that everything was going to be OK.

"One step at a time, Mum." And as Damien rested his chin on his mum's head, a beautiful green duck flew down and landed on Clara's shoulder.

"I think he likes your silver robe," Damien jested.

Clara looked closely at the duck and saw that it had the most beautiful golden eyes.

"It has a name tag," Damien said, turning over the tag around its neck. "Joy," he said, squeezing his mum.

"Permission to be happy, Mum! You've done your bit!"

The pair watched as the community came together again. People were laughing and dancing, children were jumping and chasing shooting stars and the animals played together in celebration.

The air sparkled with love and peace. The world looked like a better place.

"You know what John would say, don't you?" Clara said, smiling up at Damien.

Damien looked proudly at his mum and smiled back.

"What would John say?"

Clara pulled Damien's arm around her and cuddled into him.

"Today is the first day of the rest of our lives," she said.

Photograph by Lee Hodgess

When she's not writing, author Claire Middleton enjoys a variety of photography and art, life coaching and modelling as well as singing and dancing in any spare time she finds!

Blue Diamond Elevation, founded in 2023, brings together Claire's passions in a business designed to uplift and empower others. "I love working with spirit to spread a little magic and help people find their spark."
Website: www.bluediamondelevation.com
YouTube: Claire's School of Photography